CHAPTER 1

She was in prison and she didn't know why. Something held her down. She couldn't move her body. She couldn't turn her head. Her eyes! She struggled, but she couldn't open them. She tried to speak, but no words came. Not a sound. But she could hear unfamiliar noises that puzzled her. Footsteps and wheels. She could hear the cry of the wind in the trees. What trees? How did she know that that was the sound of bending branches and rustling leaves? Memory teased her.

She didn't know where she was. She didn't know who she was.

She was in a nightmare. She must be asleep, but if she was asleep why did she feel so much pain? Pain everywhere. Panic made her breathe harder, and she struggled in vain to break free. Something was holding her down.

There was a hand on her forehead.

"Georgie! Georgie! Georgie! Can you hear me?"

The voice was familiar, but she couldn't place it. There were more voices, at different times. Time . . . she drifted in and out of sleep, or was it in and out of unconsciousness?

In and out . . . in and out . . .

"Georgie," the voices said. "Can you hear us? Come back to us."

There were other voices. Hands soothed her, hands moved her, hands lifted her and laid her gently down again. Maybe not prison. What did she know about prisons? Why did she think this was prison?

Because her body wouldn't move? They didn't stop you talking in prison. Or walking about. Why wouldn't her voice work?

She could hear them. Who were they?

I am Georgie. Who is Georgie? She wanted to sleep, to sink deep into unconsciousness, away from noise, away from pain. The pain came and went; sometimes she felt a sharp needle stab into her skin, then the misery eased and she floated, high above the world, no longer part of it.

Some of the voices were familiar but she had no names for them. She only knew they belonged in her life. Others were strange to her, but became familiar as time passed. They belonged to people

8

who washed her face, and to the man who stung her with the needle.

There were so many voices.

Slowly, as the days went by, she recognised them and knew where they fitted into her life, though she did not know where she was or why she was there.

"When you come home we'll have an enormous celebration." That was Grandma Bridie's Irish lilt. "Girl, girl, I'd give anything to see you rush down late for breakfast, grab your toast, swallow your coffee and race out, pulling on your blazer, dragging your schoolbag . . ."

The voice broke and then went on.

"Late for the bus. Late for everything."

A hand touched her hair. She wanted to open her eyes, to explain that she could hear, but no part of her body seemed to do what she wanted. Maybe, somehow, she was a baby again. All she seemed to do was lie still and have people come and do things for her, things which she felt she ought to be doing for herself. Nothing seemed real.

She recognised Grandma Bridie first. She could see her without opening her eyes. Georgie knew she was small and a little plump, with hair that had never gone completely white, but was a mixture of dark brown and grey. Grandma who drove her little yellow Mini and always managed to crunch the gears, Grandma who was always so busy. Grandma who had come to live with them when her mother went back to work, who looked after them and the home and the animals. And Grandma who had bought the House of Secrets.

Slowly her memory returned. Her mother was a doctor. She worked in a busy practice. She had clinics. Mothers and babies. Sometimes her mother was with her, talking to her, stroking her hair and her cheeks.

Sometimes it was her father who sat beside her, always talking. He was a vet. Animals. Cats and dogs and horses. Cattle and sheep and goats. He had a surgery at home. Home was in the town. No, they had moved. They had lived in two caravans for a year, while the House of Secrets was being altered.

The House of Secrets. Bran had found it. Bran . . . he was there sometimes, talking urgently. Bran . . . they were twins. She was ten minutes older. She remembered that.

Bran played music to her, talked to her, tried to make her laugh by telling her silly jokes. Talked about school and about Liam, their little brother, who had come once and had gone away. He'd cried so much they wouldn't let him come again. Why had he cried, Georgie wondered. Bran boasted that he had grown out of all his clothes and was now nearly as tall as their father.

"I bet you've grown too," he said. "I bet I'm taller than you now, though."

She had been taller, when she could stand up and run around. Why couldn't she now?

She could visualise his shaggy dark hair, so unlike hers, even though they were twins. He had the curls and hated them. Her hair was blonde, thick and straight. His eyes were like hers, and his mouth crinkled oddly when he smiled. He was quiet, she was noisy. Unlike her, he was early for everything and worried when she was late. She wanted to look at him, but the heavy lids seemed to be glued to her eyes.

He spoke to her as though he knew she couldn't hear him. She wanted desperately to tell him that she could. But no words came. Soon she and Bran would be fifteen. She remembered that. It was important.

She drifted away. When she woke again Jenna was sitting by the bed. She was the oldest of the four children, at nearly eighteen. Georgie knew she was in bed. Jenna talked too, which was unlike her. She rarely had time for Georgie. Although Jenna seemed to live in a dream, she was always busy, always going somewhere, though no-one could keep track of her.

"Georgie," Jenna said, in a voice that sounded strange. "We need you. Come back to us. You can't leave us, Georgie." The voice was insistent, keeping her awake, preventing her from sliding back into that deep unconsciousness that formed part of each of her days. She wanted to speak, to reassure, to say, "I'm here. I can hear you. I don't know why I can't speak to you or see you. Where am I? Tell me." But no words ever came out of her mouth.

They all talked, over and over, often telling her the same old stories.

She was being dragged back to belong to them, but she didn't know where she had been.

"Do you remember, Georgie, how Romana had the little hare that had been run over?" That was Bran talking.

Romana. Who was Romana? She had a sudden vision of a laughing woman with dark hair, and a brown face tanned by the sun and the wind. She wore clothes embroidered with dancing creatures, and she lived in a caravan in the woods. Romana said she was a gypsy, a Romany, and could tell fortunes by looking at the stars.

Romana was almost part of the family now.

"Do you remember, Georgie, how you helped Lois with the ponies when the boys let them out and Lindsay was hurt?" That was Jenna again. She began to recognise the different voices and give them names.

"Do you remember Dad promised you your own horse?"

A horse of her own. She used to ride, in that other life she couldn't remember much about. Her head hurt when she tried to, but sometimes the voices talking to her brought back a flash of thought.

Running for the school bus. Lois crying . . . why was Lois crying? Standing in the stable with her face buried in Rocket's mane. Sobbing as if the world were about to end. Rocket was her favourite horse, the only one that nobody else ever rode. Lois competed with him in the local shows, and often won.

Rocket turned his wise head and stared at Georgie as she came into the stables that day. She could see him clearly in her mind. He was a big horse, with a chestnut coat, a dark flowing mane and a white star on his forehead.

"Do you remember the horses, Georgie? Lindsay, and Rocket. And all the others at the stables?"

It was her mother talking to her now. Georgie wanted to say, "I remember Rocket looking at me. Why did Lois cry?" But no words ever came.

"When you come home," they all said.

But where was she now? Not at home, she was certain of that. She was in a bed, but it wasn't her bed. The noises around her were all wrong. When there was an unusual noise, there was no birdsong, no patter of busy cats' paws as they ran

13

from room to room, no sudden bark from Troy, her brother's German Shepherd.

No dogs barking or cats crying in the little hospital at home: in pain from operations and lonely for their owners. She was beginning to remember.

For days Jenna was just a voice, and then suddenly Georgie could see her in her mind. Jenna, who was tall and slender with a creamy skin and enormous eyes, with long fair hair that she wore in a ponytail. Jenna who was always so quiet, and drifted round the house in a dream.

Slowly she put faces to the voices. Her mother told her how Liam and Bran walked Lindsay for her every morning, so she would be fit when she came home and could ride again.

Ride again. At first it was a vague idea, but one day, as her mother was telling her that Lindsay was missing her, her memory flooded.

"Lindsay's yours now. To keep," her mother said.

Lindsay, her own horse, after all these years. She saw her, remembered her in every detail, ached for her suddenly, wanting to touch the soft muzzle, to see her eager head dip impatiently into her pocket. Lindsay loved peppermints. There were always peppermints in Georgie's pocket. She felt like she would never see the chestnut mare again.

Her mother touched her forehead gently, saying, "Oh Georgie, love, can you hear us? Do you know what we're saying?" and she still couldn't answer.

There was someone else in the room. Someone who moved impatiently, who walked with brisk no-nonsense footsteps. She knew this person stood and looked down at her, and sometimes touched her. He came every day, sometimes with other people. He had no place in her past life and she couldn't imagine why he was part of this strange non-existence.

She didn't like him. She was afraid of his voice, which was sharp and harsh. He was young, she could tell from his voice, but he had no sympathy or kindness in him.

"You do realise she may never see again?" the voice said, as if she couldn't hear anything. Terror gripped her, and increased as the words flowed. "She will certainly never walk again. Goodness knows what sort of damage the accident has done to her brain."

Don't say it, her mind shrieked. I don't want to know. It isn't true.

"She's breathing by herself. She's alive, and growing stronger daily. You can't tell yet." It was her mother's voice, angry, but with a hint of desperation.

"There are times when it's foolish to hope."

"I don't give up so easily. Nature has remarkable healing powers."

"There are times when those don't work."

The footsteps marched out of the room and the door swung shut. She could hear the small slam. She could also hear her mother sobbing, and was more afraid than ever.

CHAPTER 2

The darkness persisted.

Maybe a witch had put a spell on her.

She was the victim of an enchantment, sleeping and never moving for a hundred years. Odd thoughts drifted in and out of her brain. She thought she understood something and then it floated away, leaving her feeling even more bewildered.

At times the mist cleared and she knew things very positively. Once recalled, these things stayed in her mind.

Her mother had to fit visits in between surgeries. Georgie remembered this with some relief. If there was something wrong with her, her mother would know what to do. She would know how to help her. Could she break a spell, though?

The thought teased and worried her.

Her father was a big man, who moved fast and was often noisy. Yet she never heard him come. She was only aware of him when he put his hand on her forehead and began to speak. Why did no one hold her hands? Why did her arms and legs feel so odd?

The family . . . she knew now they were her family . . . they seemed to come and go without any reason, they'd be there one minute and then gone the next. Then someone else would come. She slept and woke. Sometimes waking and sleeping seemed to be the same. Time had lost all meaning for her.

Her father talked about the dogs that came into the surgery for treatment, and about Troy, Bran's German Shepherd, who was now nearly two years old.

"She misses you, love," her father said. His hand was on her forehead, a warm and comforting hand, a moth-like touch, afraid he might hurt her if he wasn't careful. "She keeps looking in your bedroom, wondering where you've gone."

Where have I gone, Georgie wondered, but she was too tired to work anything out. She slept and woke, and listened and slept again, unaware that no one else knew when she was awake.

They came and talked to her, over and over, and went again, one after another it seemed, so that she was never alone during the day. Nights

18

were different, as the sounds changed. It was very quiet at night, sometimes so quiet that she was afraid that she was alone in the building, afraid that they had all gone and forgotten her, afraid that there would be a fire, and she would be burnt.

If she woke, she knew she was alone. The nights seemed very long and the pain came back again.

A soft voice spoke to her and the needle eased her.

Not the daytime voice. She didn't like being alone, yet she wanted to sleep and to stay asleep. She did not want to wake to a pain she didn't understand and to voices that sometimes sounded as if they had lost all hope.

"Georgie, come back to us." They kept on saying it. This time her mother's voice had an unfamiliar ring to it: a weakness in it that she had never heard before. "You've been away too long. We want you. Come back, love, do."

"Where have I gone?" Georgie wondered again, but then she felt so tired and sank back into a deep sleep, too exhausted to listen any more. When she woke up she was puzzled as it was now Bran beside her, playing some of Grandma's beloved Irish songs on his little cassette recorder.

"Where the Mountains of Mourne sweep down to the sea."

The soft haunting lines soothed her to sleep again.

One day I'll take you there, Grandma had promised her. Had it been the day before, or a week before? Or in another life that she couldn't quite remember?

When she woke they had all gone and the room was quiet. The man she liked came back again and washed her face, talking to her gently the way her father talked to sick animals. She liked the feel of her face after he had dried it, and she felt more comfortable when he combed her hair, holding her very gently.

The needle slipped in. Just a brief hurt, and then she was asleep again.

Then the dreams began. She seemed to dream the same dream, over and over. She woke briefly, which panicked her, and she was not sure whether she was asleep or awake. Then the dream began again.

At first it was wonderful. She was cycling down the lane that led to the House of Secrets. She knew they had lived there for more than a year. It had taken a year to put the house in order, to build the surgery and waiting room, the hospital for the sick animals, and to repair the stables for the horses.

The horses. The horses at Lois's stables had been Georgie's escape from the house in the town, from the noise and the sound of the beating drums from the band down the road that practised all day and half the night.

Just before they moved, Lois had to sell the stables. That was why Lois cried, she knew in her dream. There was no longer enough money to pay the bills. Georgie thought that would be the end of all her own dreams, but Grandma Bridie had found a solution.

Lois came to work for her father, and intended to qualify as a veterinary nurse. She already knew a great deal about horses. Four of the horses came with her. Among them was Georgie's own favourite, Lindsay, who had replaced the pony she rode two years ago when she was twelve. She had grown since then.

She had been thinking about all this as she cycled along. Lois had moved that day. The horses would be there when she got home. Lindsay would be in the stables at the House of Secrets.

There was a blustery wind blowing the weary October leaves from the trees. Even in her dream she felt the wind, and had to force her way against it. No-one ever cut the hedges now and they had grown so tall that they reminded her of the lanes in Cornwall where her family had spent a holiday the year before.

The sweeping branches enclosed her, cutting

off her view ahead. The lane twisted and turned. Beyond the wide verges, the ditches ran deep, and were overflowing in some places.

Twice she slowed down to ride through puddles that were almost ponds. Even so, muddy water splashed her legs, and ripples spread out from her wheels. The wind, rising to a gale, stung her cheeks, but now it was behind her, driving her on.

It had rained for several days, but now a feeble sun glittered faintly on the wet road. The wind sang in the trees, and the sound elated her, so that she knew how dogs and horses felt on windy days, when the air moved and the sky was dark with fleeing clouds. Her cheeks glowed with health, and even fighting the wind seemed like a challenge.

Only an hour or so and she would be out again on Lindsay, trotting on the grass verge, both of them exhilarated, enjoying one another's company. She had plans for Lindsay, but that was a secret she shared only with Lois. No-one else was to know about that yet.

She turned a sharp bend and the lane dipped downhill. The wind was behind her again. The road in front was clear of traffic and she picked up speed. Round the next bend came a sudden gust that almost tipped her off, and then she was on level ground, fighting the wind again. She wished the road were straight, so that the wind would stay behind her, urging her on, instead of suddenly facing her and fighting her.

She did not see the car coming towards her. It was on the wrong side of the road. She heard it, heard the scream of tyres, heard the squeal of brakes, and a second later she was flying. Now it was time to wake up, to laugh at the terror she had felt in her dream.

Crash!

This time she did wake up, wide awake. Her heart was racing, terror overriding every other feeling.

Yet she knew that the waking was unreal, as she was unable to move. She was bound, tied down, and she tried desperately to lift herself. The lack of movement had not been a dream. She realised when pain knifed through her as she tried to turn her body into a more comfortable position. She cried out. Not real words, but a scream of fear, and yet she knew, even as she screamed, that no sound had come from her mouth.

She lay there for what seemed like hours. Then someone was beside her, a soft voice was soothing her, and again a needle sank into her arm. Before she had time to consider what had happened she was asleep and the dream was repeating itself.

She woke, and this time she knew she really

was awake. She had been hurt in an accident. A very bad accident. She was covered in plaster from head to foot. There were bandages on her head and over her eyes. Her face felt stiff and sore. Every breath hurt.

She could smell flowers. And disinfectant, and there were food smells, but she wasn't hungry. She was desperately afraid and there was no-one there to comfort her.

She may never see again. She will never walk again. The voice rang in her ears, talking about her as if she were a piece of machinery, or someone who couldn't hear or think. She hated the speaker.

It hadn't been a dream. She remembered, suddenly, seeing the oncoming car, seeing the two faces of the young men driving it, staring at her, horrified, and then nothing.

She wondered how long she would be here. She must be in hospital. There was someone by her bed.

"Where am I?" It was a faraway, tiny voice, nothing like her own, but the words did come from her mouth. She heard them and so did he.

"So you're awake at last," he said. "Welcome back."

She tried to speak, but no words came. She could feel her eyes filling with tears. She couldn't stop them.

He washed her face gently. His presence reassured her.

"You're in hospital. Do you remember who you are?"

It seemed a silly question.

She was Georgina Murray. Everyone called her Georgie.

The words refused to come. Why couldn't she speak? Panic gripped her and the man beside her must have sensed it.

"Don't worry. You've had a bad time. A very bad accident. You're lucky to be here at all. It will come." Again he took her arm and the needle slipped into her skin, and she slept, and she dreamt. Only this time the dream became even more terrifying, as the speeding car swept towards her and tossed her into the air. This time she fell with a leaping jump that jerked her awake.

She screamed.

It was a real noise, a shocking sound that brought people's feet running. She didn't want to be alone.

There were hands against her face.

"You're back with us properly. What frightened you? Realising you were alone?"

"I was dreaming. I was riding my bike, and a car came and threw me into the air . . ." She stopped to consider. "That really happened, didn't it?"

They were real words. She could hear them. So could he.

"The car. It hit me!"

"It did indeed, young Georgie. But not to worry. You're getting better by the minute and we'll soon have you on your feet again. You'll be home in no time. Wait till your family come and you can talk to them again. They'll be celebrating this in a big way."

If she thought about home the pain wasn't so bad. She seemed to ache everywhere. There wasn't a bit of her that didn't hurt.

"I'm Dave," the nurse said, as he lifted her head and shoulders very gently and smoothed the pillows. "I'm your special nurse."

"I thought nurses were always women," Georgie said.

"Not any more. I'm going to give you something to make you sleep again. You'll feel better next time you wake up."

She wished she were in the big kitchen with Grandma Bridie and Jed, their mynah bird, talking nonsense at them until they longed for him to be quiet. She had forgotten about Jed. She tried to visualise his bright feathers and cheeky face, and his glinting eyes, so full of mischief.

He had been rescued and had had another life before they knew him. He said some odd things, and sometimes said some rather awful things.

The memory amused her, but when she tried to smile her face felt stiff.

Day drifted into night and then back to day again.

"They didn't come," she said as Dave washed her face and the tips of the fingers of her plastered hand, and then her other hand.

"You were asleep again. I'm afraid that was the injection, but you won't need so much today, I hope, so you should be awake this afternoon. This tube in your arm is called a drip. There's painkiller in it and antibiotics, but they haven't been strong enough for these first few weeks. The operations you had will have made you very sore. You were hit by the car; and then dragged along. You're bruised all over, and so many bones were broken."

"Operations?" What had been going on during the past days? Georgie felt frightened suddenly. She didn't want to know any more. Not yet. She wanted to ask about her eyes, but was afraid to hear the answer.

"I'm not in a ward."

"No. You needed special care. You're in one of the little side wards. You can have the radio all to yourself. Would you like it on?"

Georgie thought.

"No."

That sounded ungrateful and she added, "thanks."

27

It was too much effort to concentrate. The morning slipped away, with a nurse coming to make her more comfortable. She sounded young and happy. She told Georgie that it was a wonderful day, with the sun shining and the autumn trees bright with colours.

Four people arrived soon after the nurse left, and stood around Georgie's bed. They were voices; the young man whose voice was so harsh; a soft female Scottish voice that soothed her; a beautiful male voice that had a smile in it, and then there was a very precise voice that belonged, she was sure, to a much older woman than the others.

"Well, young lady. It's good to have you back in the world," the smiling voice said. "You worried us for some days."

"How long have I been here?"

"This is the fourteenth day. We rang your parents this morning as soon as we knew you could speak again to tell them you were off our critical list. So they'll be less worried. We're pleased with you. It's good to hear you talk."

She knew it wasn't her usual voice. It was a strange little faraway voice and she didn't seem able to think properly. The words came out so slowly.

"What has happened to me? Will my insides recover?"

"As soon as the operation wounds heal. Do you remember the accident?"

"I dreamt about it. But I don't know if it was only a dream. I remember a car coming fast round the bend. The road is very narrow there and it was on the wrong side. There were two men in it. I don't remember anything else."

"They tried to avoid you but skidded and hit you. Both your legs are broken in several places. Both arms are broken and you have several broken ribs, as well as an injured spine and fractured pelvis. You're a very tough young lady."

Broken ribs. That's why breathing hurts, Georgie thought.

The voice went on.

"Not to mention bruises everywhere and a number of cuts and grazes, as well as concussion, which is why you weren't able to talk to us. There were some internal injuries, but nothing to give us too much trouble. You are a very lucky young lady. The policemen who found you thought that you couldn't possibly survive."

"Policemen?"

"The car was stolen. The police were behind it, trying to catch it up. They saw the accident. There was a policewoman in the car who helped you. She knew first aid and was able to get an ambulance fast, which saved your life. As I said, you're a very lucky girl."

"Who were the men in the car?"

"Two silly lads out for kicks. They did try to brake but they were travelling too fast. They hit a tree after they hit you."

"Are they badly hurt?"

"Broken bones. They'll survive to stand trial. No-one has any sympathy for them."

"Are they here?"

"No. They're in another hospital."

Georgie didn't know why, but she was glad that they were nowhere nearby. She wanted to ask about her eyes, but again she didn't want to know the answer. I want to see Lindsay and Jed, and my family, she thought. I can't be blind.

She wanted to go home, wanted it so much it hurt.

The doctors went away, and she was left alone, her mind drifting. Nothing seemed real. Home was not only far away in distance, but also in time. She seemed to have been here for ever. Maybe she'd been reborn here. She didn't feel like herself at all.

She tried to imagine riding Lindsay, the feel of the saddle hard against her legs, the reins in her hands, the gentle eyes in the wise head looking back at her, the soft velvet muzzle that pushed into her hand, or dipped into her pocket, looking for peppermints.

She tried to imagine Jed with his bright colours, flapping wings and his constant pleas.

"Poor Jed. Jed's lonely."

He listened to them all and told everyone's secrets to the whole family. He barked at the cats and mewed at the dogs. He could be a ringing telephone, or a bicycle bell, or a car hooter. He startled her father's clients sometimes by saying the most extraordinary things.

Maybe she'd never walk again, never ride again, never stroke Lindsay again. Never see again. Never see the sky and the clouds racing across the sky; never see the leaves or the blossom on the trees. Never see people's faces, or Troy's wonderful brown eyes.

Tears filled her eyes. She wanted to rub them away but the plaster wouldn't let her.

CHAPTER 3

The days seemed endless. Georgie lost track of time. Sometimes she listened to the radio, but often it was too much effort. She drifted in and out of sleep. Conversation was difficult, though she liked to listen to her family. They told her about things they'd been doing but she hadn't been there with them.

Maldwyn, her father's partner, was now living in their old house. He had just married Roz, who was also a vet. Georgie should have been a bridesmaid. She remembered that. Roz sent Georgie her bouquet, but she couldn't see it. She could only smell the roses.

"Big day, today," Dave said one morning, after he had washed her face and tidied her hair. "We're going to take those bandages off your eyes. Your mother and father want to be here when we do."

"Suppose I still can't see?" The fear was back, tightening her throat, making her shake.

"Just wait and see. At the end of this week you should be able to come off that drip and to eat real food. Would you like that?"

Food. She swallowed. She was not hungry. That was the drip, they said, feeding her, quenching her thirst, keeping her alive. She wondered if robots felt like she did, stiff and uncomfortable, unable to flex their muscles, unable to eat or drink.

"You won't be there," Georgie said, suddenly realising that Dave went off duty when the day staff came on.

"I'll be back tonight."

He didn't say, "You'll see me tonight." Georgie was trying to pick up clues from the way the voices spoke. She knew that the young harsh doctor did not think she would ever see again. The other three were more cautious.

"Miracles do happen," the soft-voiced Scotswoman had said, when they thought that Georgie couldn't hear.

She listened to the radio. Music and chat. People phoning in with their opinions on a new law she had never heard of and couldn't understand. Angry people. Sad people. People who had to be cut off by the interviewer because they went on speaking for too long.

Then soft music that sent her to sleep.

"Georgie?" It was her mother's voice. "Are you awake?"

"Is it now?" she asked.

"Soon," her father said. They were silent, as if they did not know what to talk about.

"Romana wants to come and see you. They've only allowed family up to now, but they think you are strong enough for other visitors. Would you like her to come?"

"Please. And Lois. To tell me about Lindsay."

Lindsay, who she would never ride again; might never see again. The horse she had always wanted that had now come too late. It isn't fair, she thought angrily. Nothing's fair. Why did those men have to drive down that lane while I was cycling along it?

She heard the footsteps and the voices. The four doctors were there. Hands were busy about her face, unwinding the bandages.

"We'll draw the curtains over the windows," the Scotswoman said. "The room's too bright. She'll have to get used to the light slowly."

Suppose I can't see the light, Georgie thought, as the last fold was removed. She dared not open her eyes.

"Georgie? Open your eyes. Look at us."

That was her father's voice. She opened her eyes and stared up at him. He was bending over her, and she longed suddenly to reach up and kiss him, to hold onto him tightly, but no part of her would move.

She smiled at him, her face feeling stiff. Slowly, other faces appeared, at first out of focus like a bad snapshot, and then suddenly becoming more real.

Her mother bent over her. She couldn't turn her head yet. It was held still as if she were in the stocks. She had a sudden memory of herself sitting as a target at the school fete one day, while people threw wet sponges at her.

"Georgie? You can see me?"

"I can see. You're wearing the brooch I gave you for your birthday."

It was a tiny pewter brooch of an otter. His head turned to look at his tail, which curled around his body.

She felt her mother's tears wet on her face as she bent to kiss her forehead.

As she moved back, one of the men bent over her. He was a young man with dark closely-curled hair and a small dark moustache. Glittering blue eyes gazed into hers. When he spoke she knew it was the harsh-voiced man who had said she would never see or walk again. If she

35

could see, maybe he was also wrong about her walking.

"So," he said. He smiled at her, a sudden vivid smile that transformed his expression completely. She began to like him. "You're desperate to prove me wrong. Good for you. I never mind being proved wrong if it's in this way."

"I could hear, all the time," Georgie said, in that soft faraway voice that sounded more like the sigh of the wind than a girl speaking. "I could hear my mother and father talking, and Jenna and Bran and Grandma Bridie. Only my voice wouldn't work."

"It takes time," the Scotswoman said. She was young and pretty with curling chestnut hair and laughing blue eyes. "You've given us all a big bonus today, Georgie. We've all been afraid those eyes might not recover."

"At first you thought that I wouldn't either," Georgie said. "Only Dave knew I would. He said so, all the time."

"Who's Dave?" her father asked.

"He comes on at night. He talks to me, and makes the pain go away."

"He's her special nurse at night," the Scots-woman said.

"He sounds very special," said Georgie's mother.

Tonight Georgie would see what he looked like.

"Time to rest. Even the last few minutes will have made you very tired. Try and sleep," said the young doctor. "Though I doubt if you will."

They went, and the room was quiet again. Georgie looked up at the ceiling, and the light hanging above her. Out of the corner of her eye she could see the vase of flowers on her bedside table. She was propped up slightly and could see out of the window. They had drawn back the curtains as they left. The light was fading from the sky and dusk was approaching.

Outside was a patched sky with a corner of the palest blue and heavy shaggy clouds, tinged sunset red. They zipped along, sped by the wind. She had never looked at clouds in this way before. They changed shapes, some of them spreading into long narrow streamers. Others were fat, with misty edges breaking off to form smaller clouds. Some were fragile as smoke, blowing in wisps and then vanishing.

She couldn't take her eyes off the changing shapes and colours of the clouds that flared and flamed and then died away. The window was dark, with patches of light left by the houses on the faraway hill. The October leaves had gone.

Winter had come while she slept and stark branches were etched against the sky.

She knew where she was now. The fields outside her window stretched as far as she could see. Petts Hill rose up in the sky beyond the biggest field. The lights were beacons, calling to her, telling her to get well again.

She felt as if she had never looked at the world before. She looked, and looked and looked again, revelling in minute details that once she would never have noticed before. The walls of her room were a soft pink, and there was a picture of waves crashing against dark cliffs.

Her arms and legs were in plaster. It would soon be coming off, Dave said. She had seen enough hospital series on television to know that the frame beside her held the drip. The polythene bag was half full. The tube led down into her hand.

When the plaster came off she would be able to feed herself, to brush her own hair, maybe even walk round the room. She would walk. It was silly to think that she might not be able to.

She slept, and woke as Dave came in, smiling. He was older than she had thought, a neat compact man, with once-dark hair which was now turning to grey. He had wonderful brown eyes.

"I bet I don't look in the least like you imagined," he said, teasing her.

"I thought you'd have fair hair and blue eyes."

"And be a lot younger?"

"I think you look much nicer than I imagined," Georgie said.

She sighed.

"The days go so slowly. They never did before."

"They never do when you're busy. We'll have to find things for you to do, to make the time pass faster. It's surprising what you can do, even when you can't move around. You can live a whole life inside your head."

"Like what?"

Dave stood where she could see him.

"You could write stories. Have you ever thought about that? You've got a young brother, haven't you?"

"Liam. He's nine."

"Write him an adventure story. What does he like best?"

Georgie felt a giggle rising inside her.

"Pigs."

Dave laughed.

"Difficult. But let's think about it, shall we? You think of an exciting story about pigs and so will I, and we'll see who has the best ideas. Then, when you go home you can write them down."

Pigs. What did she know about pigs? She thought of Parsnip, who was a Vietnamese pot-bellied pig who lived with Mrs Grant, one of her father's clients. The children often visited her, as she lived nearby and the pig was such fun. Liam adored him, and wanted a pig of his own.

Mrs Grant lived in a big country cottage with an enormous sitting room, at one end of which was Parsnip's home, a huge hutch filled with straw.

He was an enormous fellow, with a wicked little eye that laughed at you, and a habit of head-butting you when he needed to go outside. He loved both the dogs, Cindy the Pekinese, and Tina who was a Labrador crossed with a Collie. She looked like a labrador with a fluffy coat; rather odd really.

Tina was unusually affectionate. Mrs Grant always said that Tina was a healer. When you felt miserable, she always comforted you because she was so jolly.

Maybe she could write a story about Tina and Cindy and Parsnip and Jed. Perhaps Lois would type it for her, and they could keep it a big secret from the rest of the family, who might laugh at her otherwise.

Perhaps she could save up and buy herself a word processor. Did they cost a lot of money? If she went baby-sitting . . . only, suppose she couldn't walk?

She fell asleep and dreamt that Lois had saddled Parsnip and told her to climb onto him. Parsnip was enormous, far bigger than any pig she had ever seen. As she settled herself, he gave a little buck and set off at tremendous speed. There was no mane to hold on to so she held on to his ears. She found herself in the air, with Parsnip flying over the House of Secrets.

Everyone was in the garden waving to her.

"Georgie," they shouted. "Georgie, come back. Come back."

She tried to stop Parsnip and make him turn, but he went on and on, flying higher and higher, towards an enormous moon that turned into a face waiting to gobble them both up.

CHAPTER 4

Georgie woke up just before they hit the moon. She stared up at the ceiling, wondering where she was and then remembered. Footsteps sounded along the corridor. Dave turned into the room and checked the drip beside her bed.

"I can see when you're awake now," he said, with a little smile. "Those bandages hid your eyes before and I couldn't tell whether they were open or shut. Bad dreams?"

"I dreamt I was flying on Parsnip up to the moon; it had a horrible face and was waiting to gobble us up."

He sat on the chair beside her bed. "It's scary, isn't it? Waiting to find out if you can talk, if you can see, if you can walk . . . but you can talk and you can see. It may take more time to walk."

"What do I do if I can't?"

42

"It's not the end of the world," Dave said. "My wife can't walk."

"Not at all?"

"Not one step. I used to design racing cars and she used to drive them. Then one day she had an accident in a race. I spent four years looking after her until we worked out a way for her to start a life of her own. That's why I'm here. I can help others as I helped Liz. I didn't want to stay in the racing world."

"What sort of life of her own?"

"She went back to college and took a degree in psychology. Now she counsels people who have been injured in accidents. There are so many. Road accidents, bombs, war all over the world."

"What does she tell them?"

"To work out what they can do. Not to keep worrying about what they can't do. I can't sing. I've got a voice like a croaking frog. So I wasn't meant to sing. But there are things I can do, so I work on those. I'd like to sing and have a wonderful voice, but why make an issue out of not being able to?"

"What could I do?" Georgie asked forlornly. "All I can think about is me sitting in a chair for the rest of my life. No fun of any kind."

"All sorts of fun. Reading, writing, watching. Look."

Dave picked up one of the get-well cards from

her bedside cupboard. Brightly-coloured butter-flies danced across it, framed by boughs of blossom.

"Have you ever thought about butterflies and how marvellous they are? Starting life as caterpillars, crawling, earthbound, eating leaves to keep alive, with no idea about their future."

Georgie had only thought of caterpillars as pests on Grandma Bridie's cabbages, a source of constant woe, as they did so much damage.

Dave was tracing the outline of the butterflies' shiny, fragile gleaming wings with his finger.

"One day they have a message, deep inside them, which they obey. Then they spin themselves into a cocoon. Time passes. I think they must be senseless during this time, not seeing, not hearing, maybe not even feeling anything. But changes are going on inside the little capsule."

His voice became excited as he thought about it. "Incredible changes. How does that segmented caterpillar turn into a winged butterfly? How do those magical colours develop? Think of them, Georgie, more brilliant than our man-made dyes, with a shining sparkle behind them. Orange and brown and electric blue; gold and silver, scarlet and green. Butterflies are so fragile we can crush them with just a touch, yet they are able to fly into the air, to dance on the wind, to suck nectar from a flower."

He held the card right in front of her so she could see it clearly.

"Look!" He pointed to a tiny picture of a butterfly with creamy wings, tinged at the ends with orange.

"They have such lovely names. That's an Orange-tip. It's a male. The female has black tips, but both of them are green underneath. No other butterfly is like that. Butterflies have their own areas, which the males patrol. They only live for eighteen days. They lay their eggs and then the whole process starts all over again."

Georgie had forgotten her dream. Dave looked down at her, then touched her forehead with his fingertips.

"Sleep," he said. "And dream of butterflies. As soon as you can hold a book I'll lend you mine. Pictures of Peacocks and Red Admirals, of Painted Ladies, their wings patterned with orange and brown and black and white. They are so tiny and yet they fly hundreds of kilometres to come to Britain from south-west Europe and North Africa. They are blown across the endless sea but they survive. They even manage to live through our winters. And they love thistles. There's a use for everything, Georgie."

Georgie thought of the vast numbers of tiny creatures flying across the sea, anxious to reach their chosen sanctuary so they could lay their eggs and keep the species alive. How did they do it? Why did they do it? Why not stay in one country instead of making that amazing trek across the ocean?

She would never look so casually at a butterfly again. Even the caterpillar eggs that Grandma so hated had life in them, had a blueprint that would carry them through all the changes to becoming butterflies eventually. Why were there such creatures? How did they come about?

Frogs too. They started out as extraordinarily-shaped tadpoles, then grew legs and changed completely until the adult looked nothing like its own baby.

Her mind began to spin a fantasy in which she was a caterpillar now, immobilised, unable to fly, but in time she would change, would become a butterfly, would run and walk and dance again. Would ride again.

She woke to find Dave standing beside her.

"You're getting much stronger," he said. "With any luck, they'll take the drip away today and you can eat real food. The food's good here. You'll enjoy it."

"Will you be back tonight?"

"Not for a few days. I have some time off. But

I'll be back before you leave."

"Will I ever leave?"

"Your father told me he's having one of the downstairs rooms altered to make it into a bedroom for you, so that you can look out at the garden, and have no need to go upstairs. You'll have to use a wheelchair for some time, but my guess is that one day you'll walk again. It's up to you. You'll be able to go home very soon. Your Grandma's there all day to look after you."

It was a hope to cling on to, a thought to treasure. No matter what anyone said, she would walk again.

By lunchtime the drip had been removed.

"Plaster off soon," the nurse said. "Then we'll see what we'll see."

The orderly who held the feeding cup for her at lunchtime didn't look any older than Jenna.

"I'll be a nurse one day," she said. "I left school last Christmas. I wanted to be a doctor, but I'm not clever enough."

Georgie, savouring the taste of leek and potato soup, felt a stir of curiosity. One day, she would work, and what was she going to do? Bran knew already. He wanted to be a vet like their father. Jenna was always changing her mind. First she'd wanted to be a ballet dancer, then a model. Now she wanted to learn to paint. Maybe next month she'd think of something different. Liam intended to be a pig farmer. Goodness only knew why he was so crazy about pigs. He had been taken to see Parsnip one day and had fallen in love. He wanted a pig of his own, desperately.

She was suddenly hungry for home, for her brothers and sister, for the clamour of family life, even for the quarrels. Hungry for Grandma Bridie's giant pasties and the bread that tasted better than any bread from a shop. And her cut-and-come-again cake, so-called because no one could ever resist asking for a second slice. The wonderful picture birthday cakes she made with icing on them; a horse for Georgie, a dog for Bran, a posy of flowers for Jenna and a pig for Liam.

There was too much time to think. Days at home had never been as long as these days in hospital.

She longed for visiting time, so that she could show her parents that she didn't need the drip any more. That was a big improvement. But when two o'clock came there was no-one to see her. She heard steps passing her door, people talking and laughing and then the buzz of noise from nearby wards.

Had they forgotten her now that she was getting better?

She felt more alone and sorry for herself than she had since she had arrived.

Then someone stooped over her.

"Georgie, are you awake?"

She looked at the dark face with the dark brown eyes that glinted so often with laughter. Romana was wearing a patchwork jacket embroidered with tiny birds.

"I love your jacket."

She could think of nothing else to say. She wanted to sit up and hug the gypsy woman, delighted to see her again after such a long gap. She wanted to shout and sing that she had a visitor, to say that Romana had come at last, to say that she was no longer alone. Romana would think she was daft.

"Your father has sent a message. He'll come this evening. He had a dog come into surgery that had been run over. He needs as much repairing as you do. And your mother had to go into work, as two of the other doctors are ill and there was nobody else who could go instead of her. I've something to show you," Romana said. "But it's a big secret. Just you and me. Right?"

"Right." Georgie waited, feeling as she used to as a little girl on Christmas Eve. Romana's secrets were always exciting.

"Now?" she asked.

"In a moment. Do you remember Burma?"

"Your Siamese cat?" They had all laughed at the name. Why call a Siamese cat Burma? Because she isn't Burmese, Romana had said mysteriously and had never told them more.

"Good. I've been taking her to shows and she's done very well. She's had a number of first prizes. She had kittens, two days after your accident. They're nearly six weeks old now. I've saved one for you. A little princess to become your queen. She can live with me, and I'll look after her for you, till you can do it yourself. When you're well enough we'll take her to shows with Burma, and one day she can have kittens. They're worth three hundred pounds each, so you could start saving some money for the future."

Georgie stared at her.

"Do you mean it?"

"Do I ever say anything I don't mean? Look. She's here, but don't make a noise or someone will come and tell me off for smuggling a kitten into hospital!"

She held up the tiny animal, so that Georgie could see her. It reached out a silken paw and patted her face.

The kitten was creamy-white, with the first traces of black on her nose, ears, paws and tail. One day they would be jet black like her mother's. Vivid blue eyes looked at Georgie with interest. The kitten's small plump face was smugly happy.

"Wah!" she said, at the top of an astonishingly loud voice.

A head poked round the door.

"What in the world?" It was a blonde nurse, who Georgie rarely saw. She came round to take temperatures and give out medicines, and seldom spoke.

"I thought it would cheer her up," Romana said, in a worried voice.

"It's gorgeous. Can the rest of us see it? Nobody will tell. Anyway, no doctors are due this afternoon."

By teatime Georgie felt as if she had been at a party. So many of the nurses and orderlies had slipped in to see the kitten.

The little animal was delighted with all the attention and happily sat on one lap after another. The blonde nurse closed the door and the kitten darted round the room, playing with the edge of the bedcover, catching her claw and wailing. Then she jumped onto the bed, and marched over Georgie, who couldn't feel her small weight at all through the plaster. Georgie was delighted when the kitten sat almost on her chin, and stared into her eyes.

Never had an afternoon passed so quickly since she came into the hospital.

She was sorry when everyone left and Romana

tucked the kitten into the carrying basket as tea came round. She was then free to help Georgie drink a strange concoction. She finally decided it was very sweet, very dilute cocoa, made mostly from milk. It was not easy to eat a scone either. Romana had to hold it for her.

"What are you going to call her?" Romana asked. "I waited so that you could give her a name."

"I think I'll call her Lynx," Georgie said and for a moment her eyes glinted with mischief.

"I like it. But why?"

"Because she's a Seal Point and not a Lynx Point, like Burma isn't Burmese. Seals aren't elegant so I don't want to call her that. It doesn't suit her. Lynxes are very elegant. She will be when she grows up, won't she?"

"She'll be very beautiful indeed, if she's anything like her mother. She might be twice as naughty. She's a character, this one. I picked her specially for you."

"Waw!" said Lynx, putting one paw through the opening in the basket and trying to force her way out.

"Lois sent you a present too."

She held up a large photograph of a horse's head. It had a short cropped mane and a creamy forelock of hair between her ears. The enormous brown eyes stared at Georgie as they had so often in real life.

"It's Lindsay."

"Yes, it's Lindsay. Lois had the photo taken specially for you, to make you hurry up and get better and come home. Also, she says, as you won't be riding her for some time, would you like Lindsay to have a foal?"

"Has she asked Dad?"

"He thinks it's a good idea. You'll be able to get to know it from birth and we can keep it, as there's loads of room at the House of Secrets."

"How long does it take to grow?"

"Eleven months. So if she goes to the stallion soon, the foal will be born in about a year's time. And if you can ride before then, Lois says you can ride any of the other three horses. She's busy schooling all of them and they're much quieter than they were when she had the stables, as she has more spare time now. And they aren't being ridden by all sorts of people any more. That can muddle them up."

"I'll have the plaster off soon. And then I'll know," Georgie said, beginning to worry again.

"Oh no you won't. You won't be able to do very much at all at first. It takes time to rebuild muscles and to get your strength back. But I know some of the old ways my grandfather used on his dogs and horses, and I can show these modern doctors a thing or two, believe me, Georgie."

She bent down and dropped a light kiss on Georgie's forehead. "That's to make you sleep tonight. And you can have one last look at Lynx. I'll bring her with me when I come again."

The kitten was a soft bundle against Georgie's face. She wished she could touch her, but both hands were bandaged and her arms were stiff with the plaster.

"Your parents know about Lindsay. But Lynx is our secret, so don't forget. Right?"

"Right,"Georgie said, wishing the kitten could stay, wishing that she were going home, wishing that the plaster had all gone and that she was able to move again.

The room seemed very empty when Romana and the kitten had gone. Maybe she could tell Dave about her and still keep her secret? Perhaps not. At least she could tell him about Lindsay.

A foal would be great fun.

Suddenly there was a lot to think about. Lynx growing up and having kittens of her own. And a foal to rear. She needed to know more about cats and horses, and she was now very keen to find out more about butterflies. Georgie, who had never been at all interested in reading, suddenly began to appreciate the value of books. There had always been something more interesting to do before. Dave was right. There were many things she could do, if only she turned her mind to them.

CHAPTER 5

The plaster was off at last. So were the bandages.
Georgie had expected that she would be able to
move freely, but her arms and legs refused to do
as she asked. Propped up on pillows, she could
see more of the room, and she could, just, turn
her head slightly, though the muscles felt stiff
and her neck ached.

Dave was due back that day. She had missed
him, as no one else came to talk to her when she
couldn't sleep and the nights seemed endless. She
wanted to tell him about Lindsay having a foal.
One day, far into the future, when Georgie could
walk again.

"You don't mend like magic," Sister said, seeing
Georgie's misery. "You were tossed by a car, and
then dragged. And you were cut by glass."

"How?"

Georgie could remember nothing of the accident, nor could she imagine what had actually happened.

"Nobody knows. Neither of the boys can remember anything either. They were both very badly hurt." She sighed. "So silly. One is sixteen, the other only fifteen; both far too young to be driving at all. It wasn't the first time they'd stolen a car and crashed it, but it was the first time they were hurt themselves."

The woman police constable who came to see Georgie tried to help her remember, but it was no use even trying. That made her head ache, and she began to feel panicky all over.

"Not to worry, love," she said. "People often forget what happened just before an accident. You remember more than most. You remember cycling down the lane, and the wind and the puddles in the road."

"I remember the car and the boys' faces as it came towards me. Then . . . nothing."

She tried to remember when she was alone, but found it better to think of other things. Now she had her kitten to think about. And Lindsay's foal. A year to wait, but maybe by then she'd be walking and riding and running again.

"So. You're free of all the bandages and plaster," Dave said, when he came to settle her for the night. "How does it feel?"

"More comfortable, but I still can't move. Look." She tried to lift her hand from the bed, but it refused to obey her. "Will those scars go?"

Both hands were crisscrossed with tiny red marks.

"They'll go. I promise. Look, try and move your fingers. One by one. Concentrate. Even if it's only a flicker of movement, it will be more by tomorrow, and still more by the next day. You'll be having physiotherapy soon, and they'll help you move."

"I'll never move," Georgie said. "It's worse than being a baby. At least they can move their arms and legs, and try to sit up and crawl."

"Rome wasn't built in a day," Dave said. It was one of Grandma Bridie's favourite sayings too. Everyone seemed to offer some sort of comfort, but it wasn't comfort at all.

"You have to learn patience," said Grandma Bridie's voice inside her head, as she tried to sleep. "Everything comes to he who waits." That was what the dinner lady at school said, when all the kids pushed. She had a sudden vision of herself racing downstairs, late for the bus, charging down the lane while Bran called to her impatiently from his seat by the bus door. "Come on Georgie, you'll be late; you'll make us all late."

"I promise never to be late again if I can only move," she said to herself. There were flowers all over the room, sent by her school friends, and cards on every possible ledge. On the cupboard beside her, she could see the butterfly card which Dave had moved for her. She was now lying on one side, which was a wonderful change.

She tried to clench her hand. Nothing happened. She was trapped in a body that would never work again. She hated the night, when everything was silent, except for a sudden flurry if someone was brought in on a trolley accompanied by the sound of urgent footsteps.

What brought them there in the middle of the night? An accident, a sudden illness, a heart attack? Were they frightened too? Or too ill to care, as she had been at first? It was only now that her fear was beginning to surface.

Dave looked into the room.

"You can't sleep?"

"No. I can only worry. I don't want to lie still forever. I want to do things for myself."

"It will come," Dave said. He smiled at her. "Pretend you were a caterpillar before you came here; greedy for life, grabbing at everything that came your way whenever you could, and never thinking of the future. Now you're a pupa. You're turning from a caterpillar into a butterfly. Not many people get to experience this stage."

Georgie decided Dave was a very odd man, but he was interesting.

"You have time to look. Most people never look. Do you know, one day I took my dog for a walk. He's a big yellow Labrador named Boz. We live in a street with rows of houses on both sides. Both pavements have grassy verges, planted with trees that flower in the spring. It's a very pretty road.

"Boz suddenly pawed my leg which meant he wanted me to look at something. There was a tiny squirrel on the grass verge on the other side of the road, busy washing himself, ignoring the people and the traffic going by. He was a charming little fellow, with a bushy tail and a prick-eared mischievous face."

Romana had rescued a squirrel and kept him for nearly six months, until his wounds healed. She thought he had been caught by either a fox or a cat. He had been full of mischief and was extremely destructive. Romana called him Mischief. He still came back to see her now that he was free in the woods. He played silly games of tag with Burma. You catch me, I catch you, and now we both rush up a tree.

"Boz and I watched him," Dave went on, "and then I began to watch the people who passed us. Do you know, twenty-four people came by, and not one of them even saw the squirrel. One woman nearly stepped on him." He picked up the butterfly card. "How often have you seen a butterfly and looked at it? Really looked at it?"

"Never," Georgie said. She hadn't ever been interested enough to give the little fluttering creatures a second glance. If she found a butterfly in the house she picked it up and put it out of the window. And maybe hurt it terribly, as my hands were so rough, she thought with sudden regret.

"Look at this one," Dave said, pointing to a tiny blue one. "It has an enchanting name. Cupido minimus. It's our smallest butterfly. But look at those wings. Look at the intricate veining, at the patterns, at the shape and the way they are attached to the little creature's body. They're incredible."

He stroked the picture as if it were alive.

"I can never stop marvelling at them. They live for exactly two weeks, which they spend flying from flower to flower. You mainly find them where there's limestone and chalk. They like the kidney vetch which is a tiny flower."

He put the card back on the table.

"There used to be a Large Blue, but they became extinct in Britain not so very long ago. I used to see them when I was a boy. They were fascinating. I hope we might get them in Britain again, as there are lots of them in France."

He looked down at her.

"Still not sleepy?"

Georgie shook her head. A small shake, but it was a shake.

Surprised, she did it again.

"Did you see what I did?" Imagine getting excited over being able to shake her head. But she was excited. She had moved.

"I told you," Dave said. A bell rang at the nurses' room which was just beyond her door.

"I'll come back and if you're still awake I'll tell you about the Large Blue. I'll also tell you about the Red Admiral that fell exhausted on my kitchen table."

Georgie amused herself for a few minutes thinking about a large man in a Red Admiral's uniform staggering into Dave's kitchen and falling on the table. What odd names butterflies had. So did flowers. Grandma Bridie made lists of the old names that no-one today ever seemed to use. Love in a Mist and Love Lies Bleeding. Heartsease, which was another name for the pansy; Pan's Eye. Queen Anne's Lace and Fool's Parsley. Jack Run by the Hedge. Parson in the Pulpit, which was another name for the Wild Arum, with its weird spike in the middle of a folded leaf. Romana grew snapdragons and some pretty little narcissi called Angel's Tears; and Star of Bethlehem.

Grandma fought bindweed and Fox and Cubs,

which were odd flowers with tiny ones all around them; and Mare's Tails, which the old farmer down the road called devil's fingertips, because he said they had roots that went right down to hell. Romana said they were one of the oldest plants on earth and had probably been there when there were dinosaurs. They grew far more lavishly than flowers planted in flowerbeds.

Dave came back into the room.

"I don't want to give you a pill to make you sleep," he said. "I'll just bore you to sleep. What were we talking about?"

"Large Blues."

"They always intrigued me. The female butterflies laid their eggs on the wild thyme plants. So many butterflies and insects are associated with just one plant, so that if the plant dies out, a whole species vanishes."

"And we kill them," Georgie said. "With weedkiller."

"I never use it," Dave said. "Humans spoil so many things, and don't even know they're doing it. The caterpillars hatched out, and then what do you think happened?"

"I can't even guess," Georgie said. She imagined extraordinary giant creatures roaming the fields and devouring enormous weeds.

"The caterpillars made a sort of sweet milk, which ants loved. The ants took the caterpillars to their nests. They didn't mind them eating the ant grubs, which were their food, as the ants were addicted to the wonderful nectar the caterpillars produced. It was an amazing association. You'd think it would be incredibly bad for the ants, yet they never realised it."

"Caterpillar cows," Georgie said. "You were going to tell me about a Red Admiral."

"Yes. This was a very big butterfly, even for a Red Admiral. It flew rather drunkenly into our kitchen, one very windy day. I think it had been buffeted about on the air streams. They're gorgeous, with soft brown wings striped with brilliant red."

"It's such an odd name," Georgie said. She had never thought about it before though Grandma was always finding Red Admirals in the garden.

"There are even odder names. Commas and Painted Ladies. And there are the Skippers, like the Chequered Skipper, the Silver-spotted Skipper and the Dingy Skipper."

"What are airstreams?"

"Well, there are currents in the air, just as there are currents in water. Sometimes you get something called turbulence, which is very unnerving in an aeroplane. The plane suddenly drops several hundred feet, as if it were going to fall out of the sky. Imagine what something like that would do to a butterfly. It was exhausted, and it fell on the kitchen table and just lay there with its wings folded."

"What could you do?" Georgie couldn't imagine how on earth anyone could give first aid to a butterfly. You could hardly give it the kiss of life or pump its chest!

"I got a sugar lump and put it down beside it. After a few minutes it began to move and stood on its legs. It put its proboscis out, which is a long tube-like mouth, and it held it onto the sugarlump. It squirted saliva on the lump and in a few moments there was a pool of dissolved sugar on the table. Then it sucked it up. You could see the sugar going up the transparent tube. It was absolutely fascinating."

"Did it recover?"

"About four sugar lumps later it began to fan its wings, to see if it had strength to fly. And then it took off and flew out of the window."

She was nearly asleep. Dave walked quietly out of the room. Georgie was fascinated by Dave's butterfly stories. She was becoming a different person. Maybe he was right and she was a pupa, a growing-up butterfly, and would one day be very different again.

She drifted into a world where convoys of ants carried caterpillars, far bigger than the ants were, down into their nests. There they relieved the caterpillars of their marvellous fluid. But the ants were human-size and the caterpillars were as big as whales and had udders like cows.

She woke up as the morning bustle began, and eased her legs in the bed. She felt her toes move, very slightly, only a tiny fragment of movement, but at least they had moved. She looked at her arms, which were outside the covers, and tried to move her fingers.

"That's good," said the blonde nurse who was on duty again. "You twitched two fingers. Keep trying. It won't come without an effort."

Effort. Georgie had never imagined a time would come when she would need to summon up all the energy she had just to move two fingers a fraction. She watched enviously as people came into the room, walking, talking, laughing, shaking their heads, twisting their hands, gesticulating, all without even thinking about it. They just did it.

Babies had to think about it. Had to make an enormous effort to pull themselves up. They used all sorts of things to help them, not being able to stand alone. One of the receptionists had a baby and brought the little girl to see them.

The girl was just beginning to stand. She had suddenly pulled herself up by the seat of a chair and yelled in absolute triumph and delight when she had got into a standing position for the first time ever. Georgie had never realised before what a miracle that must have seemed to the child.

Her father came in just after the doctors had finished with her on their morning round.

"Special permission, as I can't come today in visiting time," he said. "I've just been out to a mare who was having problems foaling." He yawned. "They always pick the middle of the night. But we've a lovely healthy little foal who will one day grow into a rather special stallion. He has the most distinguished parents."

Georgie couldn't wait to show him her news, which at that moment seemed more important than any foal.

"Look," she said. She shook her head, a tiny movement that she prayed he'd notice.

"That's terrific. Can you move anything else?"

"My toes, just a wiggle; and two of my fingers . . . no, three! I can feel them move, but there's not much to see."

"It'll come. It takes time and determination, and it takes effort. You can't beat the animal world for that. I didn't tell you about the lamb I went to see in April, did I? The one that couldn't move when she was born?"

"No," Georgie said. April was so long ago now, when she could still race everywhere at top speed, outrunning all her friends.

"The ewe had twin lambs. The first one began

to try to stand quite soon. He wasn't very steady, but he tried and tried until his rubbery little legs straightened up and let him move around enough to find the milk bar and start to suck. That was when the second lamb came. She moved her ears, but nothing else." Her father took her hand and held it. It was good to have him beside her, helping to pass the long lonely morning. Now the drip had gone people didn't come into the room so often as she was getting better and the nurses needed to look after those who were still very ill.

"We didn't want to interfere too soon. The ewe licked and licked and licked that lamb for nearly half an hour. She pushed her with her front legs, very gently, trying to tease the lamb into standing. Then she pulled at her scruff and lifted her onto her legs, but she fell back again. By then the lamb was moving her ears, but nothing else."

"Did she ever move? Or did she die?"

"We decided it was time to help them. We took the ewe and the two lambs into the lambing shed. We force-fed the little one, and kept on helping her to stand until she could reach her mother's udder. That ewe never gave up. She kept on pushing at her, obviously saying "Stand, stand, I'm not letting you die.""

"I'm not going to be able to move in a few days," Georgie said.

"It'll take longer than that, but it will come.

We're buying a wheelchair and as soon as we get it and the downstairs room is ready, you can come home. Romana has plans for you. She's wonderful with animals that need help to move again after an injury. Your mother and I are reading everything we can about recovery after the sort of accident you've had. Believe me, Georgie, we're all ready to live up to Granfer's favourite saying. Do you remember what it was?"

Granfer had been one of her favourite people. He had died when she was ten. That was when Grandma Bridie had sold her house and come to live with them.

Georgie remembered her grandfather talking to her when she had been trying to do something particularly difficult. She couldn't even remember what it was now.

"I'll never do it," she'd said in a passion of frustration. "It's impossible."

"There's no such word as 'can't'," she said, Granfer's thin face and white beard and merry eyes suddenly vivid in her mind. "And the impossible is only a little more difficult. You can do it if you make up your mind." He seemed to be making her try harder than she had ever tried before.

"I was five years old," she said. "I was trying to write my name and I was cross because 'Georgina' has more letters in it than 'Bran'. He only had to make four shapes and I had to learn seven, and the little g was different to the big G. I didn't think it was fair. Granfer said it would make me learn quicker than Bran, as I'd know how to make more shapes than he did."

"He was right."

It was time to plan for the future, for a future that was possible, and not to dwell too much on the fact that she might never be able to walk again.

"Can Lindsay really have a foal? Will there be enough money?"

"You'll get compensation money for your accident. I think there'll be enough coming for you to have a little bit of fun as well as all the necessary things."

He hugged her, taking care not to hug too hard. She still hurt all over, especially her ribs.

"We'll have a party for you when you come home. There's lots to see. Troy's becoming very clever. Jed has learnt a whole lot of new words, some of them a bit unfortunate. He'll make you laugh. It's not long now to Christmas. We'll find plenty of things to keep you busy, once you're home. You'll see."

Maybe it's not the way I want to be busy, Georgie thought, as her father left the room. She wished he could stay. She had planned to get into the school hockey eleven; planned to win the school medal for the Best Overall Performance on Sports Day, planned to ride Lindsay to victory at the local shows.

She looked at the butterflies on her card. She hated them because they could fly and she couldn't even move her fingers and toes more than a fraction. And then she laughed at herself, because the butterflies she was looking at were only painted ones that would never leave the page.

She lay there, trying her hardest to flex her fingers, and thought that four of them had begun to twitch this time. She was amazed at the amount of concentration she needed to do this, and soon she drifted off to sleep.

CHAPTER 6

Rain lashed against the windows. Wind shrieked round the corners of the hospital.

She hated the hospital at night when Dave was not on duty.

"I know about the black nights and the moods that overtake you suddenly," he said, often, coming in to talk to her. "I lived through them with my wife. She still has them at times. Nobody can stay cheerful or happy always."

Tonight Georgie felt desolate. She wished she could sit up or switch on an extra light. The dim glow made her feel like a little girl again, lying in her bed, afraid of the dark. There was a new nurse on, who was very young, very brisk. She bounded up and down the corridors, reminding Georgie of her grandmother saying, "Please stop walking about like a rampaging elephant," to the old Georgie as she dashed about the house.

Think about moving, Dave said. Try and twitch your fingers and toes. Keep moving your head. Each time you turn your neck, aim to move it a little bit more, to see a little bit further. Never give up.

They all said that. Grandma Bridie and Jenna and Bran, her mother and father and Romana. It was easy for them. Easy for them to come and go, to visit her and then return to their busy lives. Liam came to see her now, too, but he was always embarrassed, as if he did not know what to say to her. Almost as if he's afraid of me, Georgie thought. But I'm still me.

She didn't feel as if she belonged anywhere. She tried to imagine rushing down the field with the hockey ball, ready to shoot. She played Centre Forward. She was never likely to do that again.

Imagine vaulting onto Lindsay's back. Feel her moving, see her ears and head, feel the reins in her hands, hear Lois's voice again. "Lightly, lightly, how would you like reins pulling your mouth back, and hurting you? She should barely notice them. Just a movement, just a suggestion, just a small indication. She's a sensitive mare."

But reality was waking up and being fed her porridge like a baby. It was made very thin so she could drink it from a feeding cup. At least she could eat again and swallow properly. She never felt very hungry. How could anyone get hungry lying helpless in bed, doing nothing whatsoever?

She listened to the radio, which she preferred to television. So many daytime programmes were silly and she couldn't switch them off. If only she could get some strength in her fingers to operate the remote control.

Bran came into the room after lunch. She had lost track of the days. One followed another without any change. Even in the holidays weekends were special with her parents home. Sometimes trips were planned for them all. These had sometimes bored her but they would be great adventures now.

"Saturday," Bran said when she asked why he wasn't at school. "They let me out for good behaviour."

She wasn't in the mood for jokes. Smile they said, but she was screaming inside. Now she felt stronger, she couldn't accept that she had to just lie there.

"Twitch your fingers," Bran said. "Grandma Bridie said you could."

"Why? What good does it do?"

"If you don't try, you won't ever be able to," Romana said, drifting in through the door. "I've made you a magic cake. A little bit of this and a little bit of that and a lot of hope. It will make you able to move those fingers two inches further tomorrow."

"I don't believe in magic," Georgie said. "Nothing's magic."

"There's lots of magic. When you came in here you couldn't even see, and nobody thought you would ever see again. Now you can see us; you can see the flowers in the room and read the cards when we show them to you. You can look at the pictures on them. You can think of the friends who cared enough to go out and buy something special for you. Look at them. Flowers and horses. Otters and badgers, foxes and dogs. People who know how much you like animals."

It was more than Georgie could bear. The tears dripped from her eyes, and suddenly she was sobbing uncontrollably, unable to stop. Everyone else could get up and go home and she was stuck here, useless. As soon as they left her they'd forget her, as if they had never been there.

Romana rang the bell. A nurse came and she shooed both visitors out of the room. The needle stabbed and then Georgie slept.

She woke to find Dave sitting beside her bed. The night glow made his face remote.

"So you threw a real humdinger of a wobbly?" he said.

"I couldn't bear it. Romana and Bran . . . it's

easy for them to talk. They try to make out that there are all kinds of things I can do, if I only try. Things that have nothing to do with running around. They don't know what it's like."

"It was time," Dave said.

"What was time?" Georgie stared at him in astonishment.

"To shout, to yell, to rail against whatever fate brought you here. Time for anger. You're not the sort of girl to sit back and take things. That anger is going to help you fight back to health again."

"How?"

"Because you aren't going to be content to lie doing nothing for the rest of your life. Because those muscles can recover. There's no major nerve damage. It's going to hurt. It's going to drive you mad at times and it's going to be more difficult than anything you've ever done in your life. But you'll do it, I'm sure."

"Or die trying," Georgie said with a small laugh, remembering one of Liam's favourite expressions. "My little brother says that and Jed, our Mynah bird, is always saying it. I wish I could see Jed. What time is it?"

"Two o'clock. A long way till morning. I'm going to bring you a drink and a pill to help you sleep. Things'll be better tomorrow. You'll see."

It was good to have Dave back on duty again.

The morning dragged until at eleven o'clock, someone came into her room and spoke to her. Georgie was dozing, and she woke with a start, to look at a total stranger, sitting beside her bed in a wheelchair.

She was slim and elegant, wearing honey-coloured corduroy trousers and an aran sweater. Her blonde hair was fastened in a neat bun, and she reminded Georgie of a picture of Helen of Troy in one of her storybooks. Enormous blue eyes looked down at her.

"I'm Liz. Dave's wife. He's talked a lot about you. I couldn't come and see you before. I've been in America."

"America?"

"Yes. It's surprising what you can do, even in a wheelchair. It hasn't stopped me travelling or attending conferences. It has all sorts of gadgets to make life easier, and I can drive myself anywhere in this country in my specially-adapted car."

"Don't you mind not being able to walk?"

"Yes, of course I mind. But what's the use of agonising over something I can't change? I've had to try to make the most of what I can do. After all, most people are restricted in some way or another."

"Like what?"

"I doubt if many opera singers could ride at Olympia and win showjumping contests. I can't see the Queen dancing in a world-class skating competition, though maybe she'd love to. Your father is a splendid vet, but he probably couldn't get a first class degree in maths. He might wish he could, but he'd accept that it was impossible."

"Liam wants to be a chess champion but he never wins a single game."

"So. You settle for what you can do and you do it as well as you can. It's much better to be a first-class lorry driver than a fifth-rate cabaret singer. We all have hidden talents but some of us never find them."

"I like drawing and painting. But my hands might never work again."

"They will. Give them time. You'll have exercises to do; do them religiously, every day. You've been here nearly eight weeks now. You came in early October and it's already the first week in December. I think you'll be able to move your arms and maybe start your moving your legs before next summer."

"They don't seem to belong to me."

"It'll come. I've met so many people, some much more seriously injured than you. I remember one man who fell asleep driving his car and was appallingly injured. He was given crutches and he decided to take himself out every day round a small block of houses."

Maybe crutches were better than lying still, Georgie thought.

"The first day it took him four hours to do it. Once he'd started he had to go on, as there was nowhere he could stop. It took him over a month to reduce the time by half an hour. Five months later he went round again in three hours, with a stick. A year later he was walking eight kilometres a day, in two hours. Five years later he ran in the London Marathon and finished. He plays golf every day now."

A nurse came in with two cups of tea, Georgie's in her feeding mug. She tried to put out a hand to take it and was astounded when her arm lifted an inch from the bed.

"Good," Liz said. "That's an improvement. Dave said you could only twitch your fingers."

She took a small parcel out of a bag that was attached to the arm of the wheelchair, and opened it.

"It's a book on butterflies. Dave bought it for you. One day you'll be able to turn over the pages and read it for yourself."

She flipped the pages.

"Dave is butterfly-crazy. I didn't know anything about them when we married. Now I know so much and am as fascinated as he is. Look, that beauty is a Swallowtail. See the spikes on the wings. They're very rare, only seen in the Norfolk Broads."

Liz laughed.

"We have butterfly holidays, going where we might find a rare one. There aren't many Swallowtails and they're only around from the end of May to the middle of July. They'll disappear if they ever drain the land there. They feed on Milk Parsley, which is also rare, so if that disappears, we'll have no more Swallowtails."

Georgie looked at the caterpillars, which were green with red and black bands on them. They had bright orange horns. Liz turned the pages.

"Clouded yellows. They're so pretty. You only see them in the very south of England. Once Dave and I went to France, and there were huge clouds of butterflies, not just one or two as we see here. It was wonderful."

The pages turned again.

"Fritillaries. They have fascinating names. The Queen of Spain, the Duke of Burgundy. I often wonder who chooses their names. These feed on violets mainly." Liz sighed. "It's sad to think that if the plants go, these lovely creatures go too. They do no harm at all, and are wonderful in every way."

Georgie was startled when the orderly came in with her lunch. The morning had passed so swiftly.

"Time for me to go. I'll prop the book open for you, and you can look at it. I'm going to leave it at the Browns. They have mock eyes on their wings to confuse birds that want to eat them. The creature trying to catch them can't quite make them out, and that gives them a chance to fly away."

The wheelchair moved softly out of the room, which seemed very empty when Liz had gone.

"You'll be going home very soon," the orderly said, as she washed Georgie's face. "There's nothing much we can do for you now."

She went, and Georgie concentrated on trying to move her right hand. She was sure she had moved it over two centimetres on the bed covers.

She was going home.

"We can't do any more for you now." The words repeated in her brain.

"I'm going to prove you wrong, I'm going to walk again," she said fiercely to herself. "I'm going to ride again. I'm going to run in the London Marathon!"

It might take forever, but at least she had hope. Liz had shown her that it was possible to achieve all kinds of things, even in a wheelchair.

Long ago she and Jenna had watched a dragon-fly crawl out of its discarded skin. It had crawled up a reed, a colourless, almost ghostlike, creature, and over the next hour had developed the most striking blue colour. It was enormous. She must ask Dave what they fed on, and how long it took for the nymph to become an adult.

That night she asked Dave about it.

"The larvae, that's the nymphs, live in water for around two years," he said. "They're ravenous creatures and feed on things like tadpoles. The adults eat insects and they're mighty hunters . . . really greedy creatures, the terror of the smaller insects that live in their territory."

Georgie thought about them before she went to sleep, amazing herself as she had never before had the slightest interest in learning about wildlife.

"I'm changing," she thought, just before she fell asleep. "But what am I changing into?"

CHAPTER 7

Georgie was home. She couldn't believe it. The ambulance had taken her. It was very odd to lie down and not be able to see out of the windows. She had to try and guess where they were as they turned corners. She wondered what her new quarters at home would look like.

They had turned the house upside down. The big sitting room had been changed for her. One wall had been replaced with wide patio doors which opened on to the yard and the garden. She had a new bed. Its position could be altered by a lever on the side, so that she could lie flat, or be half-propped in an almost-sitting position.

Horses galloped endlessly on amber and brown patterned curtains and there were pictures of horses on the walls. A sheepskin rug lay in front of the fireplace.

On the other side of the yard were the four heads of Lois's horses. Lindsay was nearest to her, looking over the half door. Beyond her were Freya and Fortune and Rocket. It was good to watch Lois bustling around, cleaning out the stables, pushing the wheelbarrow past her window, waving to her as she went. To see her father walk across to the building which housed the surgery, operating rooms and waiting rooms. To see people come with their dogs and cats.

She had a new routine. Everyone raced in to kiss her good morning, and then rushed off on their own affairs. Lois and Romana called to her as they reported for duty. Lois slept in a tiny flat above the stables.

Grandma Bridie washed and dressed Georgie and vowed each day that Georgie was easier to move, that she was making movements of her own. It felt good to be in proper clothes instead of her nightie all the time. Romana had made her a waistcoat, and had embroidered Lindsay's head on it.

There were four surgeries a day, at nine, at twelve, at three, and at six, so that there was plenty to see, and lots of things to interest her, even though she was on her own most of the time. Bran brought Troy to her when he went off to school, and the dog spent much of the day lying beside her.

"If you want me, send Troy," Grandma Bridie said.

"How does she get out of the room?"

"Bran has taught her to open the door, and to come and get me if anyone says, 'Find Grandma.' We thought it would be useful."

"It must have taken a lot of doing," Georgie said. She realised that they had all been thinking about her a great deal while she was in hospital.

"Your father wrote to the people who train dogs for the disabled," Grandma said. "They told us how to go about it."

"How?"

"First of all, Bran sat in here and encouraged Troy to push the handle with her nose. Every time she did, she had a piece of chicken. She goes crazy for chicken, so she soon learnt that. Then he put her on her lead and said 'Find Grandma,' and brought her out to me and I gave her a piece of chicken. In no time at all, finding me meant she got a special feast. She can find all of us now, if you ask her. And any one of us will come to you."

"What a clever dog," Georgie said, and Troy, delighted to be noticed, sat up, her head on one side, her cheek puffed out and with the oddest expression. She went to the door and opened it, and vanished.

"Where's she gone?" Georgie asked.

"I can't imagine. Neither of us told her to go anywhere," Grandma said.

Troy bounced back into the room, her tail waving, an enormous yellow rubber bone in her mouth. She dumped it in Georgie's lap and sat waiting to be praised.

"I think she's brought you a present," Grandma said. "She's telling you how pleased she is to have you home."

Georgie wished she could stroke the dog. A moment later Troy had her front paws on the bed and her head was pushing against Georgie's hand, as if she had heard the thought. Georgie lifted her hand and stroked the soft ears.

"Did you see what I did?" She stared at Grandma Bridie.

"I did indeed. It's wonderful."

"I can't do it if I think about it."

"Then don't think. Let it happen. Troy will help you. Tell her how good she is. She knows that something is wrong, and seems to understand that she has to be gentle and must help us look after you."

"Troy's wonderful," Georgie said. She laughed as Jed, who was in his cage beside the patio doors, echoed the words.

"Troy's wonderful. Troy's wonderful. Jed's an ass," said the Mynah. He screeched suddenly and flapped his wings, shedding feathers around his cage.

She had been home a week when Grandma came in smiling. "I've got a visitor for you."

Everyone was at school, so it could not be any of her friends. Romana and Lois were busy and anyway they weren't visitors, they were practically family.

Troy barked once as a strange man came into the room.

"Don't you know me?" asked a familiar laughing voice.

"Dave! How lovely. I've never seen you without your uniform before." He looked so different in grey corduroy trousers and a bright blue anorak.

"I've brought you a present," he said, and unrolled a large poster with dozens of butterflies pictured on it. "I thought it would brighten up your room, though it's already very pretty. So this is Jed?"

"Jed's all alone. Jed's stupid." The Mynah put his head on one side, then looked at Dave and miaowed at him.

"He shows off," Georgie said.

"You'd never think he's related to the ordinary starling," Dave said, admiring the sleek black feathers, the yellow collar which started behind his eye, and the bright orange beak. "I think he's a Hill Mynah. He has another cousin, the Golden Crested, which has the most glorious yellow head."

"Do you go bird-watching as well as butterfly-watching?" Georgie asked, as Dave settled in the big armchair beside her bed and stretched out his legs.

"You find them both in the sort of places Liz and I like to visit for holidays," Dave said. "It always irritates me not to know about the creatures I see. Even starlings come in different colours. There's a Rosy Pastor . . . funny name that . . . which has a black head and wings and tail and then the rest of it is a lovely sunset pink. The Superb Starling has greeny-black wings and greeny-blue chest. Its underparts are chestnut."

He scratched Troy's ears and she leant into his hand, making a funny little noise that was almost a purr.

"But the king of them all is the Golden Breasted, which has a greeny-blue head and neck, brilliant blue wings and the most fantastic golden chest."

"We don't have many bright birds," Georgie said.

"Woodpeckers. Kingfishers. Now there's a little jewel for you. A flash of colour down by the river, where they still live in some places. But they are one of the dirtiest birds I know, with filthy nests which they don't clean."

He laughed.

"I didn't come here to talk about birds, but somehow I always seem to get distracted. They're so fascinating."

"I love watching Jed," Georgie said. "I get pictures inside my head of him which I want to put down. The way he holds his head on one side; the glint in his eye. He has a most mischievous look at times, as if he were planning what to say, and then he comes out with something outrageous. I often wonder if he really knows or if he is just doing what Dad calls parroting."

"Animals are cleverer than we think. We don't give them enough credit," Dave said. "So many people have dogs and never realise their full potential."

"Troy's clever," Georgie said. "Troy, fetch Grandma. No, Dave, don't open the door. She can."

The dog trotted across the room, butted the door handle with her nose, and then used her paw to pull the door towards her.

"Well," Dave said, in astonishment, as Troy raced out of the room.

"You rang, my lady?" Grandma asked, a few minutes later, coming into the room with a beaming smile. She carried a tray containing three cups of coffee and a plate of her home-made scones, smothered in jam and cream. Troy followed her, her tail waving happily.

"Want some?"

Grandma gave her a scone which had not been decorated. She took it delicately in her lips and lay down on the rug to eat it.

"Want some. Want some. Want some," Jed yelled, and barked suddenly. Troy, thinking there was a strange dog in the yard, sprang up and barked back. Then she looked round, embarrassed, as she realised it was only the bird teasing her.

She sank back to the floor with her head on her paws when they all laughed.

"Never mind, goose," Georgie said. "Come and see me."

Troy jumped up happily, bounded to the bed, and put her front half on Georgie's lap.

"Look!" Georgie said, as she stroked Troy very gently. Her hand was barely moving, but it was moving. "I can just wiggle my toes, too," she said.

"Terrific. It's beginning to come back and it'll get faster." Dave ate one of Grandma's scones. He watched as she cut up another and fed it to Georgie, using a fork for each piece.

"I never thought the height of my ambition

would be to feed myself," Georgie said.

"At least you can eat and swallow properly." Dave glanced out of the window. "Some people can't even do that. Is that Lindsay, the chestnut with the star on her forehead?"

"That's Lindsay. She walks over here with Lois every evening to say hello through the doors," Georgie said sadly.

"I remember one friend of ours who was paralysed for over a year. Then one day she rang us to ask us to come round quickly. She lived in the next street. She had woken up and suddenly thought she might be able to crawl. She was crawling round and round the room, on all fours. She crawled everywhere for weeks, and even crawled upstairs. Then she began to have enough strength in her legs to try and stand." Dave put his cup down on a little side table.

"What's she doing now?" Grandma asked jokily, a glimmer of laughter in her eyes. "A circus performer?"

"Not exactly. She's a very high-powered business executive for a cosmetics firm, and spends her time jetting around the world."

"In a wheelchair, like Liz?" asked Georgie.

"No. Under her own steam. You'd never guess she'd once had problems." He stood up. "Time for me to go. I'll come again, if only for those scones. They're out of this world."

"Out of this world," sang Jed, in a strange high voice.

Dave laughed.

"Oh, you," he said.

"Yoo yoo, too," said Jed.

"Time that bird was throttled," said Georgie's father, coming into the room, as Dave went out. "Can you stand him, pet, or do you want us to take him back into the kitchen?"

"I like him," Georgie said. "If there's no one else here, I can even hold a sort of conversation with him. It's a bit mad, but it makes me laugh."

"It's Christmas next week," her father said. "We're going to put the tree in here with all the presents under it, and then we can open them with you. I'm very glad you're home. I don't think we'd have felt like celebrating if you'd still been in hospital. Romana wants an hour off this afternoon. She has an idea she wants to try out. I think you're in for an interesting time."

Grandma Bridie had made a chicken risotto for lunch. Easy to eat, she said. She had put lemon, tarragon and thyme in it and it tasted delicious. So did the caramel custard.

"Have to make sure you don't get fat," Grandma said, as she washed Georgie's face. "I'm going shopping this afternoon, so don't send Troy to find me. That might puzzle her."

"Ten green bottles hanging on the wall," Jed

sang in Liam's voice, as Grandma went out of the room with the tray. Troy followed her.

"I do wish I knew what went on in your head," Georgie said. "And for goodness' sake don't sing the *whole* of that. That would drive me mad."

"Jack Sprat could eat no fat, his wife could eat no lean, gobble, gobble, gobble," said Jed, talking very fast in one of the voices he had brought with him.

"He's excelling himself," said Romana, appearing like a genie in the doorway. Her black hair was tied with a silver ribbon. It matched her silver belt, on which tiny embroidered lambs played together.

"I've had an idea."

She pulled the rug off Georgie's legs.

"Do you remember the hare that was run over and couldn't walk?" she asked.

"Yes. You used to put your scarf under his tummy and make him move his legs."

"Grandma told me about Dave's friend who learnt to crawl again and then walked. You're going to crawl."

She lifted Georgie out of the bed and laid her on the floor on her face. Georgie was too surprised to remonstrate. She felt like a sack of coal, suddenly heaved up and dumped.

Romana fastened an enormous piece of stiff cloth under her tummy, and then pulled on it.

Georgie felt herself being lifted into the air. Her legs and arms behaved as if they belonged to a rag doll.

"Now," said Romana. "I'm going to do exactly what I did with the hare. At first you won't even feel what I'm doing, but if you can get even the slightest movement into those arms and legs, we'll be making progress."

Georgie, suspended above the ground, suddenly felt her hands make contact with the floor, and she tried to straighten her arms. Romana lifted her so that she was in a crawling position on her knees, and then moved her forward. Her legs and arms collapsed again, then she dropped flat.

"The physiotherapist doesn't do that. It hurts," she said.

"Good. I'd be worried if it didn't. That would mean all the nerves had gone," Romana said. "You're *going* to walk again, Georgie, if it kills all of us in the process. This won't make things worse, I promise."

"It'll kill me first," Georgie said, half way between tears and laughter.

"Straighten your arms."

Troy ran into the room. She stared at them, puzzled, and then walked over to Georgie and licked her face. Georgie grabbed the dog's neck, and Troy moved two steps before Georgie let go.

Grandma Bridie, coming into the room a few minutes later, was astounded to see Georgie lying flat on the carpet, laughing. Troy and Romana were dancing absurdly together, Romana holding Troy's front paws, so that the dog was nearly as tall as she.

"Everybody's mad," said Jed.

CHAPTER 8

"Fight!" said Romana, over and over again. "You can do it if you try." She came every day, using her lunch hour, and was determined to help Georgie walk again.

"Do it! Do it! Do it!" shouted Jed, agitated by Romana's tone of voice. He shook his feathers all over the room, so that Grandma Bridie threatened to take him back to the kitchen again.

Do it. Move. Move a hand. Clench a fist. Wiggle a toe. Try and lift a leg. But her leg felt as heavy as a tree trunk and refused to move at all.

Move. Think about moving. Dream about moving. Was there a fraction more lift in that right arm? Did her fingers do more than creep a centimetre across the bed?

For the first two weeks the hours passed slowly.

Every day seemed endless. Even a little effort tired her at first, but then she began to feel impatient, especially when the wheelchair came.

"I've got a voice and hands," she said one morning to Lois, who brought in her coffee. "Why can't I come into the waiting room? I'd be with people then. The wheelchair will go through the door, won't it?"

"We've been waiting for you to ask," Lois said. "As soon as those hands are working you can answer the phone and take messages. It will be a tremendous help."

It was good to be among people again, even though she envied them being able to walk, able to get up and go where they pleased, when they pleased. Above all she envied Lois who, when she was free, rode out every day on one of the horses and escaped from the everyday world.

Lindsay was hers and yet Georgie couldn't do anything for the mare. Couldn't groom her or feed her. She could only watch her, longing to caress the sleek hide, longing to run out and fly into the saddle, longing to gallop away and feel the wind in her hair and to hear the speeding hooves thudding on soft turf.

When she was first wheeled into the waiting room she felt both conspicuous and shy. Even though dogs came to greet her happily, their owners seemed not to know what to say to her.

"Admire their pets," Lois said. "Ask what's wrong with them and how old they are. Say how beautiful they are."

The advice worked. It was easy enough to admire the animals that came to look at her.

She only had to say, "What a gorgeous dog. What's his name?" Or "What a gorgeous cat," or even, "What a lovely rabbit."

Suddenly she had a fund of stories. She met Joey the Dachshund whose favourite game was football. He dribbled a ball as big as himself across the garden and into the goal posts. She wished she could see him. He was a merry little dog who sat on her lap and licked her hand. He had come in for his booster injection.

His owner was a rather prim elderly lady in a tweed skirt and sheepskin coat. Georgie could not imagine her playing football with her dog, until she saw the twinkle in her eye.

"You're making it up," she said.

"I'm not. Maybe one day I can come and show you, when it isn't too busy here. He could dribble his ball across the yard."

"Promise?"

"I promise."

It was much more fun than being in her own room. Lois or Romana wheeled her into the little sitting room where they met for coffee. Her father came in, flopped down and stretched out his long legs. Grandma Bridie often joined them, bringing in scones or angel cakes or delicious little fancies that she called melting moments, which really did melt in your mouth.

"What was that big dog in the corner?" Georgie asked one late December morning. "The one with almost no fur and a wrinkled skin and an odd face. I've never seen one like him before."

"That's Mao. He comes from China. They're called Shar Peis."

There was always something new to see. A Rex cat, with curly fur, an enormous black-and-white cat called a Maine Coon. He came in on a collar and lead, walking like a dog and proceeded to entertain everyone by complaining loudly at the top of his voice. He lived with a Samoyed bitch and their owner said she wasn't sure whether the cat thought he was a dog, or the dog thought she was a cat. They played together endlessly.

Now the days sped past.

Christmas brought excitement. Everyone was racing around, hiding secrets. Georgie had her first expedition to town. Her father carried her into the Land Rover and put the wheelchair in behind them. She was able to choose presents for the family and Romana wrapped them for her.

The House of Secrets was now full of secrets, Georgie thought, as first Bran then Jenna and then Liam came into her room to show her what they had bought everyone for Christmas. Except her, of course.

The feeling of festivity excited her, helping her over a bad patch which had suddenly hit her, when she seemed to be making no progress at all.

Lois now wheeled her to the stables every day and Georgie looked on as Lindsay was groomed and fed. She spoke to the mare softly. Lindsay adored peppermints. Lois always put a few on Georgie's lap, so that Georgie could feel Lindsay's soft face against hers and enjoy a few minutes companionship. The foal was due in the summer, and that seemed a century away.

Each of the other horses had a favourite titbit, and it became a morning and evening routine to have her lap filled with tiny goodies so the horses could eat out of her lap.

Pieces of apple for Rocket who pushed against her hard, greedy for his reward. Carrot for Freya, who nibbled at it daintily. Fortune had an idiotic passion for jelly babies. Romana had made a tiny tray, divided into compartments, that sat on Georgie's lap. Each horse had its own treat and it was fun to watch them pick out their own and leave the rest.

Lindsay was always last, and Georgie spent more time with her than the others. Troy was jealous and sometimes tried to push the mare's head away from Georgie. Troy had recently adopted Georgie, much to Bran's dismay.

The Christmas tree was put up in her room. Troy watched with interest as tinsel strings and bright baubles were hung, glittering, from its branches. She sat in front of it, her head on one side, listening to the tinkling of tiny bells which jangled in the breeze when the door opened.

Romana brought the kitten in a basket to see her. Lynx tried to climb the tree when she was let out of her basket, and was brought back to lie on Georgie's bed. She purred loudly, delighted by the warmth of the soft blanket. She was growing, and her tail, legs and mask were darkening.

"I wish she could stay," Georgie said. "She's so pretty."

"She's a handful at the moment. Too much work for everyone here to look after her. Maybe later," Romana said.

Georgie watched Lynx playing with the fringe on the edge of the rug covering her legs.

"I'm sick of being useless," she shouted suddenly, startling both herself and Romana. "I can't do anything. I can't even pick Lynx up and cuddle her. I can't ride Lindsay. I can't . . ."

"Hey, hey, hey," Romana said. She caught Georgie in her arms and hugged her tightly. "Come on, that's not my girl. You're making progress. I can see it even if you can't."

"I'm sorry. It's just that I want to do so much and I can't. So I take it out on everyone else. Bran and Jenna and Liam are all angry with me. I keep shouting at them. I don't want to hear what they are doing. And I do want to hear, only it makes me so miserable because I can't. I can't go out to tea. I can't play hockey. I can't even sit up by myself. Mum and Dad and Grandma Bridie put up with me, but I'm hurting them and I don't know why."

The anger had been building up for days, and she had tried to hide it. Inside her head was a little machine that said over and over, it's not fair. Why wasn't it one of them? That made her feel even worse.

"I don't want to get mad at everyone. I just do. It's been worse since I came home. They're all busy, and I have to wait for them to come and see me, or push my chair somewhere. I have to be washed and cleaned and fed; I have to be propped up and laid down again. I can't do anything for anyone, and I feel a useless nuisance, and it's going to go on forever."

"We like coming to see you, but we all have to get on with our own lives, too, Georgie. Your parents have tried to make it more fun for you and it's good of Bran to let you have Troy so much. She is *his* dog. Grandma Bridie misses Jed. He makes her laugh."

Romana sighed and looked at her.

"You spend four hours a day in the waiting room, talking to the owners of animals that come in for treatment. Everyone has needs of their own. They can't just give up their lives for you."

Georgie still wanted to shout.

"It makes us all unhappy to think of you lying there, not being able to do anything about it. You won't be there forever. If you fight you'll walk again, ride again. It's worth trying, isn't it?"

Georgie felt worse than ever.

"Jed's lonely. Talk to Jed," the mynah said, suddenly rousing himself and peering with one bright eye at them. The other eye seemed to be watching Troy, who was scratching herself busily.

"Sing to Jed. Liam's going to be a pig stealer. Miaow." Troy barked and the kitten sat up, her eyes bright, and yowled.

Jed put his head on one side. He hadn't heard that noise before. He tried to imitate it, and it came out halfway between a miaow and a howl.

Georgie and Romana both laughed.

"I think he heard Lois telling someone that Liam wanted to be a pig breeder," Romana said. "He always manages to get things so magnificently wrong."

"Time I was going," Romana said. "Grandma Bridie will be in soon with your lunch. Lois said she'd groom Lindsay outside your window this afternoon if the weather's nice."

She went out of the room and Georgie suddenly lifted her hand and thumped her fist against the edge of the bedside table. It hurt.

She stared at it.

"How on earth did I do that? My hand worked. My arm worked. It wasn't much of a thump, but it was a thump." She had spoken aloud, excitedly. Troy came over to her and nosed her arm. She curled her fingers round the dog's ear, and stroked it gently, feeling the soft, warm, furry skin against her hand.

She could tell the difference between skin and fur. She could clench her fingers, although there was no strength in the movement. She struggled to sit up, but only her head moved.

They had to prop her in the chair every morning and after surgery was over she had to lie down. Even sitting tired her, and there was no way she could shift position by herself.

"Move, move, move," sang Jed. "Do it, do it, do it."

"Good advice," said Grandma Bridie, appearing with a tray. "One of my special vegetable soups. Nice and easy to eat. Let's be having you."

"Look, Grandma," Georgie said. She curled her fingers, making what was almost a fist. She uncurled them, and stared at them. "They moved more than they did before." She felt as if she were exploring her own body's capabilities for the first time.

"That's wonderful," Grandma said. "In no time at all you'll be able to turn the pages of a book with that hand, and maybe hold a pen – perhaps even be able to write."

"I wish it would hurry up and come back. I feel so silly, being fed like a baby," Georgie said crossly. "I hate everyone having to look after me. It's not fair on them or me. No one has time for me and I hate being alone."

"We might hate it if you were as cross as a baby with colic," Grandma said, lifting the spoon to Georgie's mouth. "I made a very special tasty meal today and there's new bread to go with it. A treat. Now be a good girl, and don't fuss. We're all prepared to help you, whatever happens. So let's hear no more nonsense."

"I'll take over," Josh Murray said, coming into the room and smiling at his daughter. "You go and feed the starving multitude. Lois and Romana are both complaining of hunger, and Sal's home. She has the afternoon off and is going to spend it with Georgie."

He took the plate and the spoon.

"Grandma has cornered all the marrow bones at the butcher to make stock for soup for you," he said. "We give the broth to all our injured animals. Romana calls it corpse reviver. It has more healing power than anything I know. We used to give it to all of you after you'd had mumps or measles, or very bad flu."

"And beef tea. And calves' foot jelly," Georgie said, remembering.

"If you do as well a cat I've been treating you'll be feeding yourself by Easter," he said.

"What happened to the cat?"

"He's a little Siamese. Well, he isn't little. He's an outsize Siamese, actually, a Seal Point, much darker in colour than most of them. He seems to go blacker every time he moults. He weighs over six kilos. A real whopper."

He finished spooning the soup and began on the honey ice cream.

"He was kept in, and rarely wandered off. The back garden had been enclosed so that he couldn't get out, or so they thought. Being clever, he discovered he could pull the wire aside at one of the posts and go exploring in the big wide world."

Georgie swallowed. Grandma had excelled herself. The thick soup was delicious, as she had promised. The honey ice cream was the most wonderful thing she had ever tasted.

"What happened?"

"He did what you did. Had an argument with a car and lost it. It broke his femur just at the point where the end of the bone enters the socket of the hip bone. I had to leave it to nature and quite honestly, I thought he'd be crippled for life."

Troy, who had been lying beside Georgie's bed, turned on to her back and rested her hind legs against the chair. Her bright eyes watched father and daughter, as if trying to follow the conversation.

"And?" Georgie asked.

"And?" said Jed, and Georgie grinned at her father.

"He started on a course of physiotherapy." He saw her startled face and laughed. "Not with anyone. He devised it for himself. He spent a week lying on his side. Then he began to try and stand. He fell over, again and again and again. And he tried again and again and again. He's been in the hospital as his owners thought he'd die. Then they said he was a show cat and, as he wasn't showable any more, they don't want him back."

"What are you going to do with him?"

"Keep him. He's only just two years old. He's lovely and he's fun and he's the chattiest animal I've ever met. Say, "How are you, Kym?" and he yowls back at you. If he's fed up he comes along and struggles up on to your shoulder. He peers into your face and talks away, as if telling you a long tarraddidle."

He laughed.

"The other day someone phoned up. Lois left the phone lying on the desk and came to find me. When I got there, the caller was having a long conversation with Kym. It was so funny that I didn't pick up the receiver straight away. I could hear this laughing voice saying, 'Well, I never talked to anyone like you before,' and Kym was answering with yowls and mews and once with a sudden loud purr."

"What did the caller say when you answered?"

"'Who was I talking to? And do you know what it was saying?'"

"What did you say?"

"'That was our Siamese cat, Kym, and he was probably telling you how awful life is just now as he's got a broken leg and can't walk.'"

"Can I have him in here?"

"As soon as Troy's accepted him and he's accepted her. At present he spits fire and tries to jump when he sees her. He can't. He falls over and that makes him very unhappy indeed. She barks at him. But after that first week he began to take some of his weight on that bad leg. Just for a second, and then he'd fall over again. Now he can go two steps on it. That's taken him another four weeks. He flops down wherever he happens to be. Two steps, collapse, and rest. Two steps, fall and rest. I've never seen anything like it. I might have written out a programme for him to follow."

"Look!" Georgie thumped her fist on the edge of the table. The sound was louder than it had been the first time she did it. "I'm beginning to move."

"That's terrific," her father said with a smile that seemed to stretch from ear to ear. "Perhaps you and Kym will recover together. I'll bring him in when Troy is with Bran. It shouldn't be too long before they make friends."

"Terrific, terrific, terrific," shouted Jed.

"Time I went back for afternoon surgery." Jed shook his wings at them. He danced for a moment on his perch, drank busily from his water bowl, picked up a piece of apple and threw it out of the cage. Then he waited for applause.

"He's impossible," Georgie said, unable to stop smiling. Jed always cheered her up.

"Comfy?"

"No. I'm sore from lying on my back all the time. I wish I could lie in water, where nothing would touch me."

"You can feel the covers?"

"Of course I can. They tickle and they itch and they're heavy."

"There's no 'of course' about it. If you can feel that then there's lots of sensation coming back.

109

You'll start to hurt; you'll start to feel as if your skin is irritating all over, and you should welcome it, Georgie, love, because that means that there's much less damage than we thought. Those legs and arms will work again."

He bent down and hugged her.

"That's the best Christmas present you could give us!"

Georgie looked at the door as he closed it. She thought how it was very odd that itching all over and feeling her skin prickle and being thoroughly uncomfortable should make anyone so pleased!

CHAPTER 9

Georgie remembered that Christmas for the rest of her life. It seemed totally unreal. Everyone was determined that she should enjoy herself, even though she was unable to move. Everyone spent as much time as possible in her room.

She was always in bed by six o'clock. She couldn't understand how she could become exhausted just sitting in a chair, but by tea time she longed to lie down.

Just sitting up for surgery times tired her, and she always had to rest afterwards.

"You mustn't expect too much too soon," her mother said, but she did expect it and fretted when her body refused to obey her mind.

Troy and Kym could now tolerate one another, though they could not be described as friends. There was still an occasional hiss from the cat and a tendency for the dog to chase. Bran had trained Troy so well that even Georgie could stop her chasing with a swift, "Here, Troy. Come to me and leave the cat alone."

Bran, who was a member of the school chess club, showed his sister how to play. She told him what moves to make for her and once even won, though she suspected he might have let her. It passed the time, as did Monopoly, which they all played one afternoon, when rain poured down outside and nobody came to surgery at all.

Georgie was surprised on Christmas morning when her mother brought in the dining trolley loaded with presents. Grandma had dressed her early and she was sitting in her wheelchair in the big warm kitchen which was the centre of activity.

"The most popular girl in the world," Sally Murray said, laughing. "Practically everyone who's talked to you in the waiting room has sent something. There are enough chocolates and sweets here to make us all fat. The policewoman who came to see you about the accident has sent you a book of British birds. It's a lovely one. We'll put a bird table outside your window so you can find out what kinds come to feed."

Dave and his wife Liz had sent her the most wonderful book of butterflies. The pictured beauties leapt from the pages as she turned them. The book he had given her before was about British butterflies. This had all the butterflies of the world. Some of them were enormous, as big as little birds.

Georgie watched in amazement as parcel after parcel was opened. A new jersey from her mother. A jacket from her father. A waistcoat embroidered with kittens from Romana. Kittens playing with balls, kittens stretching up to catch a butterfly, kittens scratching, kittens patting at feathers. All the kittens looked like Lynx.

A sweatshirt with a picture of a German Shepherd on it from Grandma Bridie.

A Celtic cross on a silver chain from Jenna. A china model of a German Shepherd from Bran. A pig money box from Liam, who had bought piggy things for everyone. His mother had a scarf with a pig on it and his father a book about pigs.

There were tiny model horses, a crystal swan with wings that glittered in the light when her father put it on the mantelpiece. The girls in her form at school had clubbed together and bought her a model horse, standing with arched head and curved foreleg, its mane and tail flowing.

Her teacher had sent her a box of games that she could play with anyone who had time to sit with her.

Breakfast was a meal full of laughter. The family unwrapped their own presents and took it in turns to spoon-feed Georgie.

Lois joined them. She wasn't able to go away for Christmas as there was no one else to help with the surgeries. Her present to Georgie was an enlarged photograph of Lindsay in a silver frame.

"That's lovely," Georgie said, admiring it.

"Now for the highlight of the day." Georgie's father vanished from the room. He reappeared a few minutes later, pushing a much more elaborate wheelchair, well-padded with cushions. He lifted Georgie into it.

"It's easier to manipulate than your old one. The back goes down so you can lie down as well as sit in it," he said, operating a lever. "It has a small electric motor which we can re-charge so that once your hands work, you can operate it by yourself."

He demonstrated.

"It will be much more comfortable. We can put it at any angle you want, and you won't need to be strapped upright. So you should manage to stay up for longer periods. Later on we'll take you adventuring," he promised.

Grandma had made a breakfast of bacon and eggy fried bread, Georgie's favourite. Bran cut it up and fed her. Afterwards he pushed her into the yard and across to the stables. He opened Lindsay's stable door, and brought the mare out. She dipped her head to Georgie's hands, which Bran filled with peppermints. The soft lips mouthed against her skin. Georgie moved her hand and almost stroked the chestnut cheeks that were so close to her face.

The wonderful smell of warm horse brought back feelings she had tried to suppress. She wanted, more than she wanted anything else in the world, to get out of the chair and jump on Lindsay's back and gallop far away.

When she was resting in her room she spent a lot of time watching Kym. He never gave up. He could now walk, though very slowly, and when he was tired he flopped down at once, wherever he was. In the middle of the yard, in the middle of the room, even on the stairs Grandma Bridie said. He seemed determined to learn to climb stairs again.

One afternoon she dozed and woke to a thumping sound. She stared at Kym, who was picking himself off the floor. He sat and glared at the armchair by the window. There was another chair beside it, an ordinary dining chair.

He sat for a long time, and then stood. He began to sway gently so that Georgie wondered what on earth he was about to do. He jumped into the armchair, but fell as he landed. He climbed up to its arm and repositioned himself and jumped to the seat of the dining chair, again falling.

Troy was out with Bran and they were alone in

the room. Jed was in the kitchen and she missed him, although sometimes she wished he'd shut up for a while when he was with her.

Kym continued to experiment. Floor, armchair seat, chair arm, dining chair seat. Over and over again. As Georgie watched she suddenly realised that, each time he jumped, he held his tail at a different angle. His tail balanced him when he landed.

Ten jumps. Twenty jumps. Thirty jumps. Surely he was getting tired, but he went on, always falling as he touched ground. He swished his tail indignantly.

Then, just when Georgie was becoming exhausted watching him, and worrying about him, he made it to the chair and kept upright. He sat, purring loudly, then climbed on to its arm. He jumped to the seat of the dining chair, again landing without falling. His tail was held almost parallel to the ground.

He repeated the sequence, and then walked over to Georgie and jumped to her lap, where he settled himself, yawning, washed his tail vigorously, and then licked her hand. She loved the feel of his rough tongue.

"You have to be very special to a cat before he washes you as well as himself," Romana said, when she told her. "They usually wash the smell of humans off them, and always off their kittens."

Georgie lay propped up against her pillows and watched the cat. She thought about his persistence, even when he must have been getting very tired. Did it hurt him when he landed badly?

She moved her hand as far as she could. Stroke Kym. Move it further next time. Stroke Kym. Stroke, stroke, stroke, stroke. It wasn't moving much. But if Kym could go on and on so could she. She'd never walk again if she didn't make any effort, and she had just seen that it was an enormous struggle.

The physiotherapist came to see her three times a week. Even she had not managed to make Georgie realise how much depended on her own efforts. So far the visits did not appear to make much difference. Her father had promised that she could go to a gym which had the right equipment for her. That was a long way in the future and would be hard to arrange. There were never many facilities in the country. The big cities had much more equipment, both in the hospitals and the gyms.

Kym didn't complain. He just got on with trying to live and enjoy himself. An hour later he was on the floor again, this time playing with a ball of paper that Bran had rolled up for him the evening before. Tap and run, in a strange sideways hobble; tap and run; in an odd slinking lope; tap and run, with a wiggle at his back end because his bad hind leg was shorter than his other one.

Clench her hand and make a fist. Clench it harder and harder and harder. There was no strength in that clench, but her fingers were moving. She was watching them as if they had no connection with her at all, willing them to move, to tighten, to bend, to stretch.

She wiggled her toes and tried to bend them. Tried to lift her foot from its flat position to an angle from the wheelchair step. It hurt. Which meant that something was working, that she was making progress. Try again and again and again. If a cat can do it, I can, she thought.

Romana came in and lifted her to the floor. Lying flat, looking at the carpet, she tried to turn her head to the side.

"Good. Keep on."

Keep on. She heard the words in her sleep. She dreamt she was walking, running, cycling, riding, even flying. In her dreams she was whole again. She hated waking up in the morning, realising that she was still trapped, a prisoner inside a body that wouldn't do what she wanted it to.

Easter came late with a burst of sunshine. There was blossom on all the trees, flowers in every garden. Her father began to take her with him on his visits. She was lifted out of the Land Rover into the farmhouse kitchens, where she could talk to different people, see cats and kittens, dogs and puppies, be pushed out to look at a new calf or foal.

It passed the time, but she always felt herself being pitied.

One day, just before the end of the Easter holidays, Bran pushed her wheelchair down to the edge of the lake. He was going to the dog club with Troy. They were practising a dog obedience display for the summer fete.

Georgie revelled in the sunshine. She loved the lake. There were swans nesting. Ducks and drakes swam busily, or dived for food, their tails waggling.

Moorhens and coots quarrelled with each other all the time, it seemed. The sun shone warmly on her face and the blue water rippled as a small breeze stroked its surface.

She did not see the boy approach. He was big for his age, a hefty fifteen-year-old in her own form at school. She had never liked him.

"Like a shove? Get moving?" he asked, and took the brake off the wheelchair.

"No. I like it here," Georgie said, wishing he would go away.

He laughed and gave her a sudden push. The wheelchair was much heavier than he had expected. It was at the top of a little slope and it began to speed towards the lake.

"Stop me. Please stop me," Georgie shouted, but the boy was staring at her, a look of total horror on his face. He tried to catch the chair, but it moved faster than he did, picking up speed, hurtling towards the water.

Instead of going to help her, he bolted, desperate to get away, terrified that someone might have seen him. He had no idea what would happen to Georgie, but he didn't want to be around when it did happen, as he knew he couldn't prevent it. Please God, let someone come, Georgie said inside her head. I can't do a thing to help myself.

She had been so happy sitting there, feeling the wind and the sun on her face. Bran had promised to come back at four o'clock and it was only three now. Her father was operating on a dog with a twisted gut which might have died if he hadn't been operated on at once. Romana and Lois would both be busy with the animals operated on that morning.

Her mother was never there during the day and Grandma had gone shopping. She wouldn't be back until five. Jenna was never in during the day and Liam had gone to his favourite farm to help with the pigs.

She looked for people, but there were only cows on the far side of the lake. There was a kestrel above her, hovering. She saw the gleam of the sun on his feathers. He seemed to be standing on air.

All these thoughts raced through her head as the chair sped relentlessly downhill. The wheels were in water, which came up to her knees. When it stopped, the jerk caused her to fall forward. She began to choke.

She was alone, sitting on the lake bottom, the water up to her neck. She couldn't move. She was too far away from home for anyone to hear her shouts, although she could see the house. She had fallen facing the shore.

If she could move . . . she thought of Kym, jumping, jumping, jumping. Though the water was quite deep it was only a short distance to the edge. But it sloped and if she wasn't careful she might slide into deeper water.

There were reeds all round her.

Could she grasp them? She was beginning to be able to grip, just a little, though she hadn't told anyone yet. Hold on and shuffle. A centimentre, another centimetre. Desperation made her move as she had never moved before. She could just drag herself, creep along, cold water all about her, her teeth chattering.

Drag herself by her hands, her fingers achieving miracles, clutching and grabbing. The water helped in one way, seeming to take some of her weight.

Grab. Move. Remember Kym. Don't give up. If I don't get out of here, I'll drown. I don't want to drown. I want to stay alive. I want to ride Lindsay, to stroke Lindsay, to see her foal, to show Lynx. Romana says she'll win prizes. I can go to cat shows even if I am still in a wheelchair.

Grab, move.

She had moved, but such a little way. She stopped, hurting all over, sure she would never be warm again. She had forgotten how cold lake water could be.

Grab, move. Over and over, struggling for her life, struggling as she had never had to struggle in all her fourteen years.

Grab, move. It was going on forever. Then, quite suddenly, Troy was galloping towards her, barking frantically, rushing into the water, gripping her clothes, dragging her towards the bank. Bran was running so fast that when he reached her he was almost speechless, panting in great wheezes.

"Georgie, hang on. I'm coming, I'm coming."

She was on the bank, soaked and shivering, with Troy racing round her, and Bran chafing her hands. He couldn't lift her. He needed the wheelchair. He waded into the lake, trying in vain to free it from the mud.

Troy's barking sent everyone to the window. They saw Bran and Troy drag Georgie out of the lake, saw the wheelchair marooned in the water. Romana and Lois and her father ran to help her.

She was in her father's arms and she couldn't stop crying. She couldn't tell any of them anything. She could only sob on and on, could only relive the terrified minutes when she felt sure she was going to drown.

Half an hour later she lay in hot water, feeling the warmth come back to her body, while Romana and Grandma fussed around her.

For the moment, her thoughts were not on the boy who pushed her, but on the fact that she had moved herself. Not very far, and that had taken nearly an hour, but she had managed to shift herself out of extreme danger and, by holding on to the reeds, had prevented herself sliding back into much deeper water.

She had never thought, during the last few months, that bed would be so welcome. It was balm to her aching body. The mattress was soft, and she was safe and warm.

Her father came in to give her some supper.

"Bran said you were quite a way from the wheelchair. How did you do it. What happened?"

"One of the boys in my class came by. He took the brake off and pushed me. Goodness knows why. I think he was just being silly and trying to frighten me. Then he got scared when he saw me heading for the water and ran away. I fell out when it stopped with a bump."

She shivered, remembering.

"I grabbed the reeds. I was so frightened, I think my hands and legs did things I didn't know they could. I managed to drag myself. I fell in front of the chair. The water was right up to my neck when I was sitting by it."

Troy was lying beside her bed. Kym was on the pillow, lying against her face, purring noisily. She was safe and suddenly furiously angry.

"It means I can't ever be by myself," she said. "I'll never feel safe by the lake again and I do love it so. There's so much to see and the time passes quickly. I can tell Bran about the birds I've seen and he finds them for me in the book."

"I've got an idea," her father said. "It may not work, so I won't tell you yet. If it does work, I think you'll be delighted."

It was a long time before she fell asleep and when she slept she dreamt that her wheelchair had been pushed over the edge of a cliff and she was falling. She woke with a jump and whistled to Troy, who heard her, pushed the door open and came to lie beside her bed.

The dog's breathing comforted her.

CHAPTER 10

Warmer weather meant that the patio doors could be open. Kym was in and out, walking round the yard, sitting outside the stables, staring up at the four heads that looked down at him with interest. Every day he roamed further, moved faster. He was making visible progress.

"If he can do it, I can," Georgie told herself.

"Time for your exercises," Romana said briskly, a week after the boy had pushed Georgie into the lake.

She sighed.

"There's an epidemic of kennel cough and another of equine flu. Half the stables are going down with it. I only hope ours don't get it. We can do without coughing horses here. We're run off our feet. Now get on yours, young Georgie."

Lying flat on her face, close to the table,

Georgie thought of how she'd been lying in the water, sure that she was about to drown. She had not been able to exercise at all for seven days. She had never been so exhausted in her life and her strength only came back slowly. For the first two days she was unable to move again, and her feelings of despair returned.

So did her nightmares.

Grandma Bridie put a camp bed in the dining room, so she could hear if Georgie screamed during the night. Troy slept beside her bed and fetched Grandma the second Georgie woke.

"Think of the water," Romana said. "What did you do that day? How did you move? The table legs are reeds. Pull on them."

Georgie reached out her arms and gripped the table leg. She pulled herself along, her knees and feet pushing against the ground. She felt as if her arms were being pulled out of their sockets.

"I moved all of five centimetres," she said in despair.

"You moved. Pull. And again. And again. And again."

"Pull, pull, pull, pull," screeched Jed, in one of his madder voices. "Do it. Do it. Do it. You can, can, can."

Georgie collapsed and giggled helplessly.

Jed, encouraged by the laughter, began to sing "Amazing Grace." Kym, offended by the noise, stalked through the patio doors into the yard and Troy barked.

Jed barked back.

"What is going on?" Grandma Bridie asked, arriving with lunch for all three of them. "It's a good job there isn't a surgery. Our clients would think we were all mad and go somewhere else."

"It's just Jed, helping with my exercises. He sounded so funny, and so silly."

Romana lifted Georgie back into her chair.

"Jed's funny. Jed's funny. Jed's lonely. Poor Jed."

"Jed's impossible," Grandma said, handing a plate of egg and cress sandwiches to Romana.

"Impossible," sang Jed, suddenly chattering like an angry magpie at Kym, who had come into the room and was sitting eyeing the food. Troy, who knew better than to pester people while they were eating, lay with her nose on her paws beside the patio doors, and watched every mouthful.

Georgie could now hold food but couldn't lift it to her mouth. She practised daily with a pencil, trying to lift it to her face. She hated being fed. She hated being washed. She hated the daily struggle to dress her.

"Be glad you can eat, can swallow, can digest," Romana said, when Georgie complained.

Only Romana and the animals knew that she could now hold a pencil, could write and draw if she wanted, though not very well. It was a secret. Georgie liked having secrets. It gave her a feeling of power. She had no power at all otherwise. Her chair had been cleaned up since the accident, but she could not yet work it by herself.

She couldn't get up and walk. She had to wait until someone was free to take her.

She could now turn over the pages of a book if it was on her lap. The words she wrote were recognisable although her writing was as sprawly as a six year old's.

"Don't tell them yet," she pleaded to Romana. "Just in case it goes wrong. I don't want everyone to know. It's like announcing that you're going to pass an exam with flying colours and then going on to fail miserably."

Romana, who read horoscopes, who never walked under a ladder and who always saluted a single magpie, understood perfectly. Georgie didn't want her horoscope cast. She was too afraid of what it might say.

Romana brought a sketch book and an exercise book with her. Georgie practised writing and drawing. Little comical drawings of Kym. Kym walking. Kym jumping. Kym balancing himself using his tail.

Jenna and Liam and Bran were back at school. Their lives went on. Her life seemed to stand still. One afternoon Lois wheeled her into the kitchen.

One of the police dogs needed an operation to remove a cyst from above his eye. Jed was watching the wicket gate that led from the yard to the road, his head on one side. Only moments before she thought he said something daft, recognising his expression. The late surgery would soon begin, and she hoped Lois would remember to wheel her back into the waiting room.

A big bearded man walked across the yard, with one of the most beautiful German Shepherds she had ever seen pacing regally beside him. He must have come in for his booster. There couldn't be anything wrong.

His black saddle gleamed. The sun brightened the gingery fur of his legs and chest and the sides of his cheeks. His muzzle was black, and there were black stripes on his forehead which looked like enormous eyebrows.

He turned his head, saw Troy and stared at her.

"Daft dog. Daft dog. Daft dog," shouted Jed in Jenna's voice. Georgie prayed that the man hadn't thought she was speaking.

The man turned too, and looked across the yard at Georgie, then flicked a finger to his dog, which followed him immediately. They vanished into the waiting room. No one else came. It was a small surgery. Maybe her father might even have time to come and talk to her.

The minutes ticked past. The woman who had gone in first came out, without the basket. The cat had stayed in. Georgie hoped desperately that it wasn't dying, or didn't need some awful operation.

At last there was only the bearded man and the German Shepherd to come out, but time passed and nothing happened. Georgie began to worry. Suppose the dog had bitten someone and come to be put down? Or killed a sheep? Or had some awful problem, like leukaemia, and her father was tied up all afternoon. If he had to put a healthy dog to sleep he would be miserable and wouldn't come in to see her.

He'd go for a long walk and no one would see him until the next day.

She looked at the clock. The hands had only moved two minutes. Time was standing still again. It was a pity dogs didn't have hands, then Troy could turn the radio on for her. Romana had forgotten and Grandma was out. Jed was asleep, his head tucked under his wing. Kym was asleep, pushed up into the hollow under her arm. Troy was asleep, though her ears moved and Georgie knew that she would be up and alert at the slightest sound.

There was a butterfly outside her window, fluttering in the breeze. She hoped Kym wouldn't wake up, as he would catch it. Or try to. Did butterflies feel fear? Did they realise that there was a hunter stalking them? It was a Red Admiral. Sometimes they seemed to hide in the house and come to life during the winter.

It hovered outside the window, looking for flowers that weren't there. It loves teasel, scabious, ivy and buddleia, Dave said. Grandma had planted several tiny bushes, but as yet they had not flowered.

Five minutes had passed. The afternoon stretched in front of her, endlessly boring, with no one to talk to and nothing to do. She couldn't try and sketch as Romana had taken away the pad. Even if she had left it, Georgie needed it put in front of her on the tray, balanced across her chair arms, and she needed her arm lifted into the right position.

"Georgie!"

She woke, blinking, as her father touched her arm gently. The bearded man was beside him, his dog sitting in front of her. Troy was watching from her corner. She must have been told not to move, as she would be longing to greet the newcomer.

"This is Major Simms," her father said. "He has a surprise for you."

"Hello, Georgie," the big man said. He had

grey hair and a grey beard. The blue eyes set deep beneath grey bushy eyebrows looked at her kindly.

Georgie stared at him, not knowing quite what to say or why he was there. He smiled at her.

"I'm a dog trainer. Of a rather special kind. I train dogs to help people who can't always help themselves. This is Khan. From now on he's going to be your eyes and your ears, sometimes your hands and certainly your protector."

Georgie couldn't believe it. Her own dog. This beautiful animal was to be hers. She loved Troy, but always felt guilty because she knew that Bran didn't really want his sister to monopolise his dog. Now she needn't.

"Khan," Georgie said. She had forgotten that Kym was lying curled against her, almost hidden by the rug. As the dog pushed his nose into her hand, the cat emerged, stared in horror, spat loudly and bolted.

"They'll get used to one another," Major Simms said.

Georgie stroked the muzzle above the soft cold nose that pushed into her hand. The dog looked at her out of wise brown eyes that seemed to understand he was now to be hers. He knew so much more than even Troy.

When she could walk again . . .

The thought filled her with utter despair.

"Will you take him away from me when I can walk again? I don't want him if it's only for a short time."

"He's yours for always. It will be quite a few years before you are as fit as you were before. You may need him for a long time yet. I hear you had a bad scare. He can also protect you when you're alone."

"How can he protect me?"

"I'll show you."

Major Simms made some kind of signal and Romana came out of the waiting room door. At once Khan stood up and barked at her.

"Friend, Khan," the man said and the dog stopped barking and watched as Romana crossed the yard and came into the room.

"You have to say 'friend' fast, if it is someone you want to see," the man said.

"Major Simms has taught a lot of dogs," her father said. " He suggested some time ago that you should have your own dog, and he began to train Khan for you. His dogs always come to me when they need treatment. We've known one another a long time. Then we won't be depriving Bran of Troy all the time. He's been very good, sharing her with you, but he is trying to train her for competition, and she does spend most of her time with you and not him."

"But how do I know what Khan can do?"

Georgie asked. "I need to be able to give him the right commands."

"I'm staying here for a week. I'll leave Khan with you each day. I'm just down the road, at the pub. I'll be with you all day and I'll show you everything Khan can do. Meanwhile, just remember to say 'friend' the minute you see anyone you know well and trust. Once he knows all the family and everyone who comes to see you, he won't bark at them."

"What would he do if I didn't say 'friend'?"

"He'd keep circling you, barking, making sure the person didn't come near," Major Simms said. "He's a very safe dog. He's just over eighteen months old now. He's been trained since he was ten months old. Before that he was puppy-walked, the way they do the Guide Dogs for the Blind, by a lady who took him everywhere. He's been in boats, in aeroplanes, to the seaside, to the fair, to the market, through sheep fields and cattle fields. He knows about road crossings. He's as well-trained as any guide dog but he comes with extras."

By tea time Khan had fetched her a pen and a paperback book, and had pulled the new length of cord that now operated the light switch. She couldn't understand why her father had had it put in. It was nowhere near her bed or the place where her chair usually stood. Now she realised that this was one of Khan's favourite tasks, as he switched it on and off several times and then turned with laughing eyes and mouth to look at them for approval.

"That was a piece of show-off naughtiness you'll have to guard against," Major Simms said. "On, Khan and leave it on."

It was an 'I-mean-it-or-else' voice, and the dog at once pulled the cord and the light flashed on. He came back to sit beside Georgie's chair.

"Remember he's just a dog, and he may not always do as you want instantly. Or may have his own variation. You have to be firm. Any problems and I'll come back."

He flicked a finger and the dog came to stand beside him.

"Your father needs to show me where the dogs can empty themselves without causing problems," he said. "I'll take Troy with me too, and they can have a game and make friends. You won't be alone. I'll be back before your Grandma goes to make the family meal."

Her father and the Major came into sight, the two dogs frisking in front of them. Kym had retreated to the stables. Horses were safer than strange dogs. Every now and then Georgie heard his complaining yowl and every time he made the noise the two dogs turned round trying to see him.

It was late when Major Simms finally left her. He spent the evening showing her what Khan could do and making sure that she said 'friend' very quickly when people she knew came into the room. The family used the door from the hallway, and it was easy for them to forget that a strange dog was there.

"It'll take time for you both to get used to one another," the Major said. "I think Khan knows he is staying here. I'll bring in his bed and his rug."

Troy was now with Bran, and her bed had been removed.

It was exciting to have something new to think about. Georgie began, for the first time since her accident, to feel that she had a future after all.

CHAPTER 11

One bright Spring day Jed was put in his cage outside the window. He mocked the birds, imitating them, and miaowed at Kym. As Major Simms came into the yard he suddenly shouted, "Friend, friend, friend," in Georgie's voice.

The Major, coming in at the door, stared at Georgie.

"How on earth could you see me?"

"I couldn't."

"Then why did you call out 'Friend'? That could upset all Khan's training."

"I didn't. *He* did." She nodded towards the Mynah who began to sing in a reedy voice.

"Twinkle, twinkle, little star,
How I wonder what you are
Up above the world so high
Kissed the girls and made them cry."

The major laughed.

"He's very funny, but I'm afraid he can't be anywhere near you when you and Khan are working together. If he keeps giving the dog commands, it will confuse him terribly."

"Khan," said the bird, in Major Simms voice. "Switch on the light."

The big dog stood up and walked over to the cord and tugged. The sunlight was so bright that the electric light barely showed.

"See what I mean?" the Major said.

Georgie had woken up that day feeling miserable. Her low spirits plummeted even further. It wasn't going to work. They'd take Khan away from her. She had not noticed Romana coming into the room with a tray containing cups of coffee and Georgie's favourite chocolate biscuits.

"We'd thought of that problem," she said, putting a cup and plate in front of the Major. "Jed's coming to live with me. If he's anywhere within earshot of the dog, he'll muddle him. Lois was going to have him, but you can hear him from her room above the stables. My caravan's right away from here, up in the woods."

"I don't want Jed to have to go away because of me," Georgie said miserably. "It's not fair."

"He knows me well. He won't be far away. We can push you up to see him, and he can come back and visit. Your dad and the Major spent so much time working out what Khan could do to help you. It would be a shame to waste it. He's been trained to suit you, not anybody else."

Khan, sensing her unhappiness, pushed his head into her hand. Why do I have to feel like this? Georgie wondered. One minute I know I can do everything I want, in time, and the next, it all seems as if nothing will ever go right again.

"I've got nothing to do all day and nor have you," the Major said. "So we're going on an expedition and a picnic. Khan's coming with us and we'll see how we fare in a completely different place."

Like her father, he drove a Land Rover. He lifted her into the passenger seat, and put her wheelchair and a big hamper that Romana brought out, into the back. Khan jumped in and lay down.

Georgie's mood lifted as they drove miles into the country. Through lanes blazing with blossom, past moors where the gorse flamed back at the sun. They had been driving for over two hours when they dropped into a narrow, windy lane. They came to a long low building that she suddenly realised was made up of line after line of stables.

"My brother and his wife live here," Major Simms said. "Nessa, my sister-in-law, matches mares that have lost their foals with foals that have lost their mothers. Mostly racehorses. Here she comes now," he added.

A tall woman with a mass of blonde hair tied back in a black velvet ribbon came towards them, smiling.

"So this is Georgie. Come and meet Vance, my husband."

She laughed as Khan danced up to her, tail waving, and tried to take her hand in his mouth. "I thought you'd grown out of your baby ways. Grow up, son. I bred him," she said. "His mother is already very useful indeed. She fetches and carries, and can even take buckets of feed to the mares, providing I don't fill them too full."

Major Simms lifted Georgie into her wheel-chair. They passed rows of stable doors with wise heads looking out at them. Beyond it was a field where several mares were grazing, with small foals beside them. A gate opened into a walled garden where the sun beat down fiercely.

At the far end a man was lying in a long chair, a large umbrella shading him. A lovely German Shepherd bitch lay beside him. She stood up when she saw them and came over and nosed Khan. Suddenly the two of them were playing an absurd game of tag all round the flowerbeds, never putting a paw on any of them and keeping to the grass and the paths.

The man smiled at them and whistled. At once

140

the bitch left her game and stood beside him.

He smiled at Georgie. His intense blue eyes were like his brother's but his face was much thinner. His hands looked almost transparent.

Georgie looked at him, dismayed.

"Didn't Craig tell you? How like him!" He smiled at her again. "I broke my back in a hunting accident a long time ago. I'm used to life in the slow lane now. I can do all kinds of things with Hexa's help. I can also work a computer and keep the accounts. It's surprising what you can do if you try."

Major Simms brought over a small garden table.

"We brought food," he said. "It was very short notice but I couldn't waste such a beautiful day. This place doesn't look half as attractive in the rain, and I knew Vance would enjoy a visitor."

"I asked Craig to bring you as soon as he could. I want to show Hexa off," Vance said to Georgie. "Then you'll begin to find ideas for training her son. I think Khan could be cleverer than she is. He came here for three months at the end of his puppy-walking, and Hexa and I began to train him before Craig trained him specially for you."

Georgie was beginning to feel ashamed. She could sit up now. She had started to move her legs and her hands were already much stronger.

"Lift, Hexa," Vance said and the dog went

over to his chair-bed, took a lever in her mouth and shifted it, so that he could change his position. He was now propped half-sitting. Khan had dropped to the grass by Georgie's chair, panting after his romp.

Romana had sliced a roast chicken. There were two plastic bowls, one containing a green salad and the other a rice salad. There were Grandma's crusty rolls and butter and scones, and little jars of jam and cream.

Nessa added ham and tongue and more bowls of salad, a dish piled high with fruit, a large meringue covered in raspberries and swirling high with cream.

"Wonderful what you can do with freezers," Vance said. "I still have to rely on Nessa to feed me. Hexa's never learnt to do that!"

He looked across at Georgie, who could find nothing to say. She felt as if she had ventured into unreality, far away from everyone she knew, among total strangers who lived in one of the most beautiful places she had ever seen.

"Give her some of your speciality," Vance said. "I'll guarantee she's never tasted anything like it."

Nessa fed her husband, while Georgie had the Major sitting beside her, feeding her as if he had done it every day of his life. Georgie's hands still wouldn't lift from her lap to her mouth. She hated being fed, especially away from home, but somehow, watching Vance, who also seemed to have problems with swallowing, she no longer minded.

She concentrated on the food. It was impossible to identify the background taste. There was rice, prawns and anchovies, some kind of fruit that she had never seen before, and a sauce that was both sweet and sharp at the same time, with a tang to it that made her want to eat more and more.

The sun baked down on them and Major Simms brought more of the huge umbrellas. He put them into the little troughs that had been built for them. The dogs stretched out in the shade cast by the high wall.

Several cats basked in the sun, quite unafraid of the two German Shepherds.

"They're stable cats. They earn their keep by killing the rats, as does Tommy," Nessa said, as a small Jack Russell trotted into the garden and flopped down beside the two big dogs. Both of them nosed him and then relaxed again.

"People are so busy these days that it's difficult to find anyone who has time. It's good to have someone young to visit us. Craig must bring you again. How old are you, Georgie?" Vance asked.

"Nearly fifteen."

"You'll get your strength back, and make up for what you've missed in life. I had twenty-eight

143

years before I was paralysed. Luckily Nessa's a strong person and makes the most of whatever happens to her. We already had training stables for racehorses. It didn't take a lot of effort to convert them, as I did the training, and the place was already set up. I still have my horses. I can even bring them to me."

He smiled mischievously at her.

"Hexa, fetch Blaze."

The bitch vanished. Georgie thought Khan might follow her, but he stretched out at her feet with a deep sigh.

"Why Hexa?" she asked. "And what's Nessa's real name? I've not met anyone called Nessa before."

"Hexa's German for witch. She really is a little witch, of the most delightful kind. Enchanting and bewitching. Nessa's name is Vanessa and she hates it."

Hexa came back into the garden. Following her round the corner of the stables was a big chestnut hunter, who moved quietly and serenely down the path behind the dog. Hexa held a leading rein in her mouth. The horse came to Vance's bed, ducked his head, and took an apple out of a large bag that was hanging from the post by the man's head.

The soft nose pushed into the hollow of Vance's neck, who moved a hand gently to stroke him.

"I can just manage a stroke, and I can feel his warmth and softness. Their muzzles are so velvety, and their eyes so wonderful. I can hear music and voices; hold conversations and I can see the world around me. There are compensations. You learn to make the best of what you have."

Will I ever do that? Georgie wondered. Settle for not being able to run around and live like other people?

Vance was still talking.

"I can't hold anything. No grip. Blaze is my old hunter. Would you believe he's over twenty now? A grand old fellow, aren't you, son?"

The horse dipped his head as if nodding. He had the longest lashes that Georgie had ever seen on any horse.

"He was seven years old when we fell. Both of us, him on top of me. He couldn't help it, poor fellow. There was a low wire at ground level and we couldn't see it. Even in those days there were folk who wanted to stop hunting." He sighed. "People mean well but they don't know what they're doing. Foxes do so much damage and if there are too many they starve to death anyway as there isn't enough food for them. I don't like hunting them; I don't like hearing a goose dying as the fox takes her. Life isn't black and white, Georgie. It's a mixture of colours, mostly greys.

145

Just sometimes there are vivid flashes of scarlet and red and blue, to lighten our lives."

"Do you believe there's sense to it?" Georgie asked. She couldn't believe there was any purpose whatsoever in being so badly injured that she could scarcely move.

"Lying here, with so much time to think, I see links; pathways; directions. Khan was born. Because of me, Craig trained Hexa, as he had trained other dogs. I had two other dogs before her. Khan, he said, was to be for someone special. If you'd never cycled down that lane . . . if those boys had never taken that car . . . if you could still walk and run and play games, you'd never have had Khan, and I'd never have had the pleasure of meeting you. Or of tasting your grandmother's superb scones and jam, and cream!"

"You're laughing at me," Georgie said.

"No, I'd never do that. When you're my age, which is nearly forty-two, you might understand what we have said today better than you do now. We all need experience, or we never grow up at all. Some people never do grow up. They learn nothing however long they live and make the same mistakes at seventy that they made at seventeen."

"There speaks the old man," Major Simms said, interrupting.

146

"Craig's my baby brother. A whole two years younger than I am. You'd never think it, would you?" Georgie looked up at the Major, who grinned at her. He was a big man, with broad shoulders. Vance laughed. "Even in my heyday he made two of me. He takes after our father, who was a big burly man. I take after our mother. She was tiny and very slim, but packed with energy."

Georgie thought, pondering all he had said.

"Where have the events in your own life led you?"

"Craig's trained over thirty dogs now for people in various degrees of immobility. And our thousandth mare was given our thousandth foal this week. All those babies will go on to live active lives as a result of what we do here. It's much more fun than training racehorses which we did before my accident. We're doing much more good for so many more people now."

Nessa, who had cleared away the dishes, returned carrying a saddle and bridle. She put them on Blaze, and then she looked at Georgie.

"We've been wondering," she said. "Are you game for a small experiment? It might hurt a bit, but it would be worth it."

"Worth a try?" Vance asked.

Georgie nodded, though she had no idea what was about to happen. The Major began to push her chair towards the stables. They crossed the yard towards one of the stables. There was a ramp, which ended in a platform almost level with the horse's back. He pushed the chair up the ramp and braked at the top. Then he lifted Georgie and held her tightly, her legs dangling uselessly on either side of the saddle.

"You don't weigh much more than a butterfly," he said. "Feel safe?"

Nessa was standing beside Blaze, holding him still.

"So long as you don't let me go. I'll crumple up like a rag doll if you do," Georgie said.

She felt a small thrill of long-forgotten excitement. Maybe if she could sit on Lindsay, maybe somehow she could ride . . . maybe . . .

"Feel good?" Nessa asked.

"It feels wonderful. Just to be here, on his back." It was also a little frightening. The ground was a long way below her. Blaze was a much bigger horse than Lindsay. Suppose the Major let her go? Suppose she fell? That might be the end of all hope of a full recovery.

It was months since she had had such a view, looking down on the world from a height. Ever since her accident she had looked up at everyone towering above her.

She could see over the garden hedge, and look down towards the lawn where Vance was lying.

He saw her and lifted a hand slowly, making a small motion that she knew was a wave, a gesture of greeting.

"You're lucky," Nessa said. "You can sit up. Vance can't and never will. He couldn't sit on a horse, even with somebody holding him in position." She looked up at Georgie. "Do you realise that Craig has just let go of you?"

Georgie thought she was going to fall, but the strong arms were round her again.

"You can do more than you think," the Major said. "I suspected as much. Have you tried to sit by yourself?"

"No," Georgie said, suddenly wondering how much more effort she could make if she tried harder. Did she accept too easily that she couldn't do things?

"I can come over to the House of Secrets and we'll see if you can sit on Lindsay and ride around a little," the Major said.

"I won't be able to." She dared not hope. The disappointment would be so much greater if she found it impossible.

"We'll see."

The Major lifted her down and settled her in her chair again. Even that small effort had exhausted her. He lowered the back rest so that she was almost reclining and wheeled her down the ramp.

There were clouds across the sky. Nessa unsaddled Blaze and led him into his stable. She fetched her husband, wheeling his chair into the house.

"Tea inside and then we must be off. I promised we wouldn't be late home. Your parents were worried as you haven't driven so far before. I promised to make sure you weren't overtired."

There were egg and cress sandwiches and more scones, jam and cream and a sponge cake so light it almost floated. The three dogs watched from their posts, but never fussed or bothered.

"I can't come tomorrow," the Major said. "I'm driving to Scotland to bring back a foal whose mother died when he was born. There's a mare just arrived, grieving for her own baby. In two days time, they'll both be happy again. But I will come."

"Do you live here too?" Georgie asked.

"I have my own flat just down the road, but I work here. Nessa couldn't manage on her own. The dogs are my priority but I help with the horses and do anything else that's needed. I enjoy it immensely as animals are always rewarding to work with. Like Vance, I came upon my way of life by accident."

Georgie remembered a previously puzzling conversation that her grandmother had had with Romana recently.

"The poor man lost his wife a few years ago.

She was killed in a plane crash on her way home from visiting her mother in America. Luckily he's so busy looking after his sister-in-law's animals and that invalid husband of hers that he has made a good life for himself."

She had not been feeling well enough that day to ask who they were talking about but she knew now that it had to be Major Simms.

Georgie found the journey home exhausting. She was not used to sitting up for so long.

"Something to talk about for days," Major Simms said, a couple of hours later, as he lay Georgie on her bed. "You'll feel very tired, but you'll be much better tomorrow."

Georgie nodded. She ached all over and, as Vance had said, the bumping from travelling often hurt.

"Light, Khan," she said and watched happily, as the dog walked over and pulled the cord. Light flooded the room. She looked at the clock. Half past ten. She hadn't been up so late since her accident.

Her mother came in to put her to bed.

"Have a good day?" she asked.

"A wonderful day," Georgie said. She was asleep almost before her mother had left the room.

CHAPTER 12

In the next few months the Major brought added excitement to Georgie's life. They had a conspiracy between them. Whenever he was free, he called in and took her out in her chair. Nobody realised that she did not stay in her chair. Later, when she had more use in her hands, she would be able to operate the chair herself, but at the moment she did not have enough strength.

Lois became part of the conspiracy. Lindsay couldn't be ridden as she was now in foal, but as soon as the Major and Georgie disappeared, Lois saddled Freya and rode down the lane.

Freya, who was just 14.2 hands high, was on the border line between a horse and pony. This depended, Georgie was sure, on whether she stood up straight or drooped a little. She was lovely to ride, with a smooth flowing gait. It was easy for the Major and Lois to help Georgie into the saddle.

Just being on Freya's back made Georgie feel whole again, even though she didn't have enough strength in her legs or in her arms to do more than be a passenger. The Major held her firmly, his arms giving her security, while Lois led her.

"Don't tell anyone," Georgie begged them. "One day, I want to ride into the yard by myself, and surprise them all."

The chair had its limitations. They couldn't push it in fields as the ground was too rough, and were forced to keep to good surfaces, or it was quite impossible. The only wild place she could visit was the lake, as there was a path.

Freya could walk in the fields. She could take Georgie along the river bank, where she could see kingfishers and the quick little divers standing on the boulders and ducking under the water, flapping their wings jerkily.

The Major knew as much as Dave about wild-life, and their walks became explorations. They found a mass of White Admiral butterflies at the edge of the woods that bordered the field by the lake.

"They are there because nobody manages the woods round here," the Major said. "White Admirals used to be rare in the days when big landowners kept an army of men to look after their property. They need honeysuckle to feed on and that wasn't allowed to develop as it smothers everything. Now it's all over the place and so are the butterflies."

"Why White Admiral?" Georgie asked. "It's nearly all browny- orange."

"It's the band of white on the wings that gives it its name. The females lay their eggs on the honeysuckle. They only live about four weeks. A very short life. Just time to ensure the next generation is born."

Each journey was a little longer than the last. Georgie was delighted because she was out on Freya, and did not realise that Lois and the Major were gradually encouraging her to do more, and to travel further. No one in the family realised that Georgie was out on Freya. They all thought the Major was pushing her in her chair and that Lois was simply exercising her horse.

There were other landmarks, when Georgie looked back. But she did not realise at the time that events were causing her to try harder to use unfamiliar muscles.

Life began to be worth living again.

CHAPTER 13

Georgie was now able to feed herself. She ate her breakfast, but then watched everyone else rush about their business, and felt more frustrated than ever.

Khan pushed his head against her, she gripped his collar, and he began to pull away from her. She let go and he pushed again.

And again.

"What do you want?" she asked. She gripped again and Khan pulled away, looking at her as if trying hard to tell her something important.

It was difficult to hold on to the collar when he pulled. Suddenly she realised that this was a new and different form of exercise. If she tried to tug against the dog, her hands and arms would strengthen.

Pull. Pull. Pull.

It became a game between them when nobody else was there. Georgie enjoyed her secrets and longed to surprise them all. Over and over again, Khan would invite her to tug against him as if he knew he were helping her. She felt the strength returning to her muscles. Each day the time she could struggle without too much pain increased, until she was able to resist his full strength.

One morning in early October he tugged so hard that she stood, but overbalanced, and fell. He was out of the room immediately, barking for someone, anyone, to come and help her.

Lois raced in, and lifted her back into her chair.

"How did you do that? Have you hurt yourself?"

"I'm fine," Georgie said, elated by the fact that she had actually stood on her own, even if only for a few seconds. "I tried to move the chair and fell, that's all. I didn't hurt myself."

One day, she'd astound them all by walking across the room. She wished she could think of a way of tugging with her legs as she did with her arms, with Khan helping her, of course.

The Major was now pushing her feet into the stirrups. Slowly, she began to feel that she could press down and almost stand up when on horseback. Press. Push. Grip.

Lindsay's foal was almost due. Maybe next

week. If only Georgie could be there when it was born. She and Bran were now fifteen. He brought school work home for her. She was busier now than she would have believed possible only a few months ago.

One afternoon, sitting in the little office that Lois and Romana also used as a sitting room, she managed to start the engine on her chair by herself. She drove it across the room to the word processor.

It was on, but the screen was blank. She began to type, slowly, with one finger, delighted to see the words appearing on the screen.

"That's fantastic," her father said. She hadn't seen him come into the room. "I'll buy you your own computer. You can use it to catch up on your school lessons, and to write to your friends. Maybe play games on it, to pass the time."

She didn't need computer games to pass the time. She was out on Freya several days a week. Khan invented games for both of them. She could now throw things for him to fetch, which he did endlessly, with enormous excitement. His favourite thing was a piece of drainpipe.

Time flew past. Kym and the dogs kept her company, unless Bran was at home, in which case Troy went with him. Khan seemed to interpret her thoughts.

Georgie had never imagined life could be so

interesting, even though she was still not able to walk. Nobody knew that she could use Khan to pull her to her feet, could stand for almost a minute, and then sit herself back in the chair. Each day she was able to stand for a few seconds longer.

She was alone in her room one afternoon in early November, concentrating on her lessons. She would soon be able to catch up, and maybe even take the exams. A year late, but she would still take them.

She looked out of the window. The horses were in the big paddock except for Lindsay who was in a tiny piece of fenced-off grass where they could keep an eye on her. Lois had wheeled Georgie over to see her the day before.

"It won't be long now," she had said. "Look at her udder. It's enormous and it looks waxy. There's a tiny drop of milk. She's all ready for the baby."

Lindsay was stamping a hoof and yawning widely. The foal might be coming and there was nobody around. Suppose something went wrong? Her father was out, visiting a farm. Grandma Bridie had gone shopping. Romana wasn't due in that afternoon.

There were two hours before evening surgery. Georgie counted the horses in the field. Rocket was missing, so Lois had taken him out for exercise. She was on her own.

Georgie felt desperate. She had never seen a mare foal before and was sure something was wrong. Lindsay was almost crouching and a small swelling appeared under her lifted tail.

She rolled, and then lay on one side, making odd noises.

Georgie did not stop to think. If only she could start her chair. She had managed it once before. Her strength seemed to come and go, quite unreasonably.

Try.

Move that arm.

Lindsay needs you.

Press down. Press harder. Press. Click.

The chair began to move. She had to steer it. She suddenly felt terrified. Suppose she couldn't handle it? Suppose she drove out of the patio doors and across the yard and hit the opposite wall?

The patio doors opened by pushing a button which Khan could press. The dog did as he was told and sat watching her, his head on one side, his eyes puzzled. Georgie had never gone out alone before. The way was free. Yesterday she had held the reins, and for the first time had managed to ask Freya to turn left and turn right. It couldn't be any more difficult to steer the chair.

She drove out of the patio doors, down the

ramp and across the yard. She couldn't manage the telephone. If only she could phone Romana who would come fast. She couldn't lift it. It was just three o'clock. Bran and Jenna wouldn't be home for another two hours. Grandma might return soon, but then again she might not. There was no surgery until five. No one would hurry. It was a half day and there were only two surgeries instead of the usual four, to give everyone a chance to take time off between eleven in the morning and five o'clock. Usually there were surgeries at twelve thirty and at three o'clock as well. If only there had been today.

No use being an 'if only' person, Romana often said. Make it happen, Georgie. You can.

Only she knew how much it hurt at times to make that extra effort. It was going to hurt now. Her arms would ache after trying to steer the chair. She knew how to do it. Could she do it?

Lindsay rolled again, and whinnied, as if asking for someone to come and help her.

Now. It's up to me, and no one else, Georgie thought, and gripped with all her strength. The chair rolled down the ramp and into the yard. Turn towards the little paddock.

Her father had said only that morning that he didn't think Lindsay would foal today. Otherwise Lois wouldn't have gone out and left her.

There was a slimy bundle protruding from the

mare. A leg was visible inside it. Was this what was supposed to happen? Lindsay suddenly stood up again, the bundle now bigger. Suppose the foal fell from her and injured itself? Shouldn't she be lying down?

Lindsay whinnied suddenly and then lay down again. The membrane around the foal had broken and Georgie could see two tiny hooves, lying side by side. Did it always take so long? Please, somebody, come. Make sure she's all right. Suppose the foal dies because nobody's here to help?

Gradually the bundle became larger and larger, the mare making enormous efforts to bring the baby into the world. Georgie sat helpless. She wanted to get out of her chair, to open the tiny gate, to get close to the mare. Lindsay needed her.

Khan could open the gate.

She whistled to him.

When he had pushed up the latch and pulled the gate open, she told him to lie down. The wheelchair wouldn't go through the gap and might frighten Lindsay. She pulled herself up on the fence rail and, holding on to it, she managed to stagger along and through the gate.

Lindsay was lying on the grass.

Georgie crawled across to her. There was so much ground to cover. It had looked such a short distance from the house, but now she actually had to move herself it felt like a mile. Crawl and flop. Crawl and flop. She felt like an enormous unco-ordinated baby. Crawl and flop. She was out of breath, her arms hurt and her legs hurt and she wanted to lie down and cry.

Don't be so stupid, she told herself. The grass was damp under her hands. It had rained the night before.

She collapsed by the mare, her cheek against Lindsay's head.

She began to talk.

"Good girl. Clever girl. Go on. It's all right."

Maybe she shouldn't be there, but she needed to be there and was sure Lindsay needed her. She had never realised birth could be so difficult.

Suddenly she felt Lindsay's body heave violently and there on the ground lay the foal, wrapped in the thick membrane that covered him like a glistening sheet. Lindsay lay as if she had no more strength in her.

The foal had to breathe. Georgie could reach its head, but did not know what to do next. Should she put her hand into his mouth and clear his breathing passages? Could she manage that? While she was wondering, the mare pushed across her and began to lick the foal's head. Slowly, the membrane vanished and there on the ground lay the tiniest foal Georgie had ever seen. His ears flickered, his small tail wagged, and he tried to stand, but fell. He sneezed, and sneezed again, taking in air with great gasps, trying to learn how to breathe properly.

Georgie forgot her aching legs and arms. She forgot the damp ground that was making her uncomfortable. He was a miracle, a wonderful little miniature horse, so perfect he seemed unreal. Lindsay's eyes were soft as she washed him lovingly, encouraging him to try to stand, aware that this was her baby.

He was a rich chestnut colour, with a white blaze on his nose and a white star on his forehead. Lindsay had the star but not the blaze.

Georgie had no strength left. She managed to sit up and lean against Lindsay's shoulders and watched the foal struggle. Within minutes he was standing at his mother's shoulder, then hunting along her underside, looking for milk.

Georgie heard the clatter of hooves as Rocket came into the yard. Lois saw her, put her horse in his stable, and raced across.

"Georgie, how did you get there?"

"I don't really know. I was afraid that something was wrong. I don't know what I thought I could do, but I just had to be with her . . . it was taking so long and I didn't know if the foal was all right. I made the chair move. Lois, I worked the chair by myself!"

She suddenly realised what she had done and,

though she had no strength left to get up, she was elated.

Lois put an arm round her and helped her back into the chair.

"Everything's fine," she said. "Isn't he gorgeous? We'll have to think of a name. Want to go in?"

"I want to watch him for a bit. Close to."

Lois went for warm water and a sponge to clean the mare from the birth. She brought gruel for her to drink, while the foal, who had fallen again, made several attempts to stand on his rubbery legs, that splayed in all directions.

He tried determinedly until at last he managed to stagger several small steps. At last he was up, his legs under control. He was drinking greedily, his busy sucking noise causing Khan to sit with his head on one side, intrigued by a new sound.

The baby could not feed for long without collapsing. He couldn't understand why his legs wouldn't work as he wanted them to all the time.

"I know just how he feels," Georgie thought, wishing she could recover her strength as rapidly as the baby had found his.

"Surgery time. You'll have to go in," Lois said, as a thin rain began to fall. "You can watch from the window until it gets dark. I'll have to put them in then."

Georgie could hardly eat her tea, she was so enthralled.

"I'm going to call him Miracle," she said, when her father came in after surgery, to wheel her into the kitchen for their evening meal. "And look, I can move myself."

She showed him how she worked the chair.

"Take it slowly, love," he said. "Your hands might manage it for a little while, but if you go too far and your strength fails, you'll be in trouble."

"I can get to the kitchen," Georgie said. "Just keep close to me, in case."

She led the way, her father following. It was a moment before anyone realised that she had got there on her own. And when they did, their praises were all she could have wished for. Her father cut her meat for her, and after that she could feed herself.

Maybe next term she could go back to school, if her father could take her and her chair. She could get around the ground floor. Anyway, none of her lessons at school was upstairs.

It was another step forward, but there was still a very long way to go.

CHAPTER 14

By the beginning of December she was standing alone without needing to hold on to anything or anyone. She was walking two steps on her own, feeling like a baby beginning to toddle. She could hold on to the edge of the table and creep along it. She could reach for a book from the bookcase.

Romana and the physiotherapist both knew she could stand, but neither realised she could actually move herself, with extreme difficulty, more than just a step.

The Major knew. She could now walk from her wheelchair towards Freya, and was even able to use her arms to help haul herself into the saddle. She had ridden a few yards by herself, but was still afraid to allow the Major to let go of her, or let Lois give up the leading rein.

If she did fall indoors, she could pull herself up

by Khan's collar. She would manage to get to her knees and then drag herself back into the chair. She took care never to try when anyone might come into the room.

Her family were delighted by the progress she was making. She intended to give them the surprise of their lives at Christmas. Christmas became a deadline. The day when everything would go right, the day when she would prove to herself that she was no longer confined to the wheelchair, that she would be back at school, able to cope, even though she knew that it would be months before she was fully mobile.

One day soon . . .

It became a litany, a prayer, a dream to be fulfilled. She had to work to make the dream come true. Often after her ride on Freya she ached so much that she felt she would never be able even to crawl out of her chair.

"Do it," the Major said, over and over again, reminding her of Jed encouraging her, so long ago now, it seemed.

She spend more time with her family now and less time alone in her room. Her computer gave her the excuse for solitude and nobody realised quite how often the Major called in. Then he had to go away for a few days. There was snow and then ice, and it wasn't safe to go out. Her rides on Freya stopped.

The days became drearily long again, and her father would not allow her to drive her chair across the yard to watch the foal, now growing fast and full of energy and fun. He loved people, who all loved him, of course. He came to be stroked and petted, rubbing his small head against Georgie when Lois helped her to stand. Not even Lois realised that Georgie could do much more than keep herself upright.

Christmas Day came at last. Georgie felt like a little girl on Christmas Eve, only this time she *was* Father Christmas. She could now eat like a normal person and could help whoever dressed her. One day she would be able to dress herself again. She could wash her own face and hands.

Breakfast first and then to open the presents. Major Simms had taken her out shopping in her wheelchair and Romana had helped her wrap all the presents except her own. Lois helped with that.

Romana and Lois joined the family as neither had families of their own.

The big sitting room looked like a Christmas grotto, the tree glimmering in the corner. Kym and the two dogs watched it warily, almost afraid it might blow up on them. No one would guess that Kym had ever been injured. He could jump and run and climb trees again.

Georgie hugged herself impatiently as everyone

unwrapped their gifts. She couldn't wait, but she intended to keep her own secrets until the very last moment.

"I've got something to show you," she said, when at last the room was quiet and the wrappings had been tidied away.

She whistled to Khan. He came to her and she hooked her hands into his collar. As he pulled, she stood up. Khan sat and looked at her, as she began to walk towards her father. One step. Two steps. Three steps. The room seemed enormous and she wavered and almost fell, but the table was beside her and she steadied herself.

They were all staring at her in amazement and then, as she walked on, everyone began to smile. Ten steps and she was there. She fell against her father, who caught her in his arms and hugged her so tightly she thought she'd never breathe again. She sat beside him on the settee, while everyone talked at once.

"Why didn't you tell us?" her mother asked, hugging her too.

"I wanted it to be a Christmas surprise. Major Simms and Lois have been helping me. As well as everyone else, and Khan made me exercise my arms even when I didn't want to."

Bran was dancing round the room, singing.

"Georgie can walk. Georgie can walk. Georgie can walk."

"There's something else," Georgie said. "Only you'll have to come outside."

Lois followed Georgie as she drove her chair out through the door into the yard. They had ramps everywhere for her now. Freya was already saddled.

Out of the chair and a few steps across to the mare. She gripped the saddle and heaved herself up. Lois helped her to hoist herself into position. She rode out of the gate and down the lane, the family watching in total amazement.

"I have my own surprise," Lois said, as a young man, who was standing by the gate, stepped forward and took a photograph. "I thought you'd all like that for your family album."

Georgie, feeling rash with all the excitement, rode down to the end of the lane, turned and rode back again. It was only a hundred metres, but she felt as if she had taken a giant step into the future. In a few months' time she'd be riding properly again. Her legs were beginning to grip. Her hands were much stronger.

"When you can ride a mile Lynx can come home, as you'll be able to look after her," her father said. "I think that you can go back to school, too. They're willing to make provisions for your wheelchair. We've measured all the doors, and there's plenty of room. They'll make ramps into the cloakroom, and once there, there's no problem with the corridors."

The week after Christmas Lois came in smiling, and handed Georgie the local paper.

She stared at it.

There was the photograph of herself on Freya, and a big headline saying:

Crash Girl Makes Good.

She read on.

"Georgie Murray, aged fifteen, daughter of our well-known veterinary surgeon Josh Murray and his equally well-known wife, Dr Sally Murray, has made a miraculous recovery.

"Thought at the time of her road accident to be unable ever to walk again, Georgie is now able to walk across a room, and has full use of her arms and hands.

"She had been keeping this a secret from her family but had an even bigger secret, as, helped by Lois Thomas, one of her father's veterinary nurses, and Major Craig Simms, Georgie has begun to ride again.

"She has put her convalescence to good purpose by writing a story for our Christmas competition about her Siamese cat, Kym, himself badly injured in a road accident. The story, illustrated by delightful cartoons, describes his fight back to health which, Georgie tells us, inspired her to try his methods of natural physiotherapy.

"Georgie says she has a long way to go to full recovery. But it is obvious that with her determination, she will soon be living a normal and rewarding life."

"They never told me," Georgie said.

"We felt it would be more fun if we kept it a secret," Romana said. "I told you, didn't I? The house makes its own secrets and goes on making them. There are many more to come yet, you'll see!"

They all had secrets. Even Liam, but none of them guessed that during the next few years, Liam's secret was to astound them all.

Homecoming by Cynthia Voigt
£3.50

Dicey made her announcement to James, Sammy and Maybeth: "We're going to have to walk all the way to Bridgeport." But they had no money and the whole world was arranged for people who had money – or rather, for adults who had money. The world was arranged against kids. Well, she could handle it. She'd have to. Somehow.

Dicey's Song by Cynthia Voigt
£3.50

Still troubled about her mother, and anxious about the three younger children, Dicey seems to have no time for growing up – until an incident at school shows her what to do.

A Solitary Blue by Cynthia Voigt
£3.50

Jeff has always been a loner, ever since his mother walked out, leaving him with his taciturn and distant father. Then his mother invites him to Charleston. For one glorious summer, Jeff is happy, before his dreams are shattered.

The Runner by Cynthia Voigt
£3.50

Bullet Tillerman has little interest in anyone or anything except running. But this is the 1960s, and with racial war at home and the Vietnam War abroad, Bullet's beliefs have to change, particularly when he's asked to coach a new black runner at the school.

Some Other War
Linda Newbery

Seventeen-year-old twins Jack and Alice have their lives mapped out. Jack is a stable lad at the Morlands' country house, and Alice is chambermaid to Madeleine Morland. Had it not been for the First World War, they might have stayed there all their lives. But the war changed many things, and brought Jack and Alice independence from the rigid social structure of the times.

Jack joins up with the first flush of enthusiasm, and is sent to the trenches. Alice continues at the Morlands', but as the casualties mount up and it becomes obvious the war will not be over by Christmas, she feels she must do something to help and begins working as a nurse.

Linda Newbery's novel accurately and sympathetically portrays life at the time of the Great War through the eyes of young people.

£3.99